Jack Vance
Gold and Iron

Jack Vance

Gold and Iron

Jack Vance

Spatterlight Press Signature Series, Volume 9

Published by Spatterlight Press

Cover art by Peter White

ISBN 978-1-61947-130-6

Spatterlight Press LLC

Spatterlight
P R E S S
340 S. Lemon Ave #1916
Walnut, CA 91789

www.jackvance.com

FOREWORD

Nowadays we would call this a post-colonial novel. Of course, that term didn't exist in 1952 when Jack Vance published *Gold and Iron* (under the title "Planet of the Damned") in the magazine *Space Stories*. Although I will note the curious symmetry in Vance's novel finally appearing in book form six years later, now renamed as *Slaves of the Klau*, at almost the same moment when Nigerian author Chinua Achebe released his *Things Fall Apart* — acknowledged in recent years as the defining work of post-colonial literature. The two novels share many similarities, but Achebe's story is a staple of college course reading lists, while Vance's book has long been out-of-print.

Yet Vance was there first, dealing with these issues before they entered the literary mainstream. The other defining text of postcolonial writing, Edward Said's *Orientalism*, was still a quarter of a century in the future when Vance wrote his story, and *The Empire Writes Back: Theory and Practice in Post-Colonial Literatures* by Bill Ashcroft, Gareth Griffiths, and Helen Tiffin wouldn't be published until 1989. Vance, in other words, was working on his own off his personal compass of social values, yet he already grasped the key elements of the movement in his Cold War pulp fiction tale.

Here we find a tale of colonization told from the standpoint of the subjugated population. Here we encounter the inevitable bloodshed and turbulence as different colonial powers battle for supremacy, with the indigenous population watching on as bystanders in the larger conflict. Here we see the resulting social instability — "things falling apart" in Achebe's Yeats-inspired words — and the alienation of the local populace as traditions and norms are destroyed by more 'advanced' concepts.

But with one big difference: Vance's story is set in the future and spans intergalactic space. The target audience for *Gold and Iron* (the name Vance himself preferred for the novel) demanded fast-paced action, and Vance knew how to maintain a madcap momentum, even as he explored ideas and concepts more suitable for social studies and political science classrooms. (In these pages, Vance gives himself an outlet for these speculations by making his romantic lead, the lovely Lekthwanian lass Lelianr, an interplanetary anthropologist.)

Vance artfully deconstructs concepts of primitivism and cultural hierarchies, but in a playful way that you won't find in any academic text. One of my favorite scenes in *Gold and Iron* follows our hero Roy Barch, a colonized Earthling, on a first date with the entrancing Lelianr. She is interested in exotic customs of human society, and Barch promises to take her to a "voodoo orgy." Instead, he brings her to a nightclub (the real-life Hambone Kelly's) to hear the Yerba Buena Jazz Band. The chronology makes no sense — this hot traditional jazz combo had flourished on the West Coast in the years following World War II, and had already disbanded before Vance published his novel. But the idea of bringing an extraterrestrial researcher to a jazz club gives Vance a choice platform to mock notions of the noble savage and other highbrow pretensions.

Jazz was almost as important to Vance as science fiction. In his memoir, he recalls that his Aunt Nellie Holbrook, who lived on Filbert Street in San Francisco, was so opposed to jazz music that she refused to use the word — and when forced to refer to her nephew's music obsession relied on the code term 'zazz' instead. The first record Vance purchased was "Daybreak Express" by Duke Ellington (by coincidence the first jazz music I played for my oldest son Michael as an infant — he enjoyed the band's emulation of the sound of a steam locomotive). Vance expanded his jazz knowledge by listening to the Camel Caravan radio broadcast on Thursday nights, where he heard the Casa Loma Orchestra, the prototype for the swing orchestras that would dominate America's nightlife in the late 1930s.

Even before that time, Vance rode a Harley-Davidson motorcycle. He worked as a bellhop and elevator operator at the Olympic Club. He learned how to play kazoo and cornet. He enrolled at Berkeley, and wrote for *The Daily Californian*, and started to write science fiction stories. This was more than a decade before the rise of the Beat movement, but Vance was always ahead of his time. As a young man, he defined bohemianism in an age of conformity.

This story first arrived at the bookstore in the form of an Ace double, a series of popular paperbacks that offered two novel-length sci-fi tales in a single thirty-five cent volume. If readers flipped *Slaves of the Klau* over and upside down, they could read Vance's *Big Planet*. Yes, the concept seems cheesy, and the garish covers made it doubly unlikely any grown-up would be caught in public with an Ace double in hand. But for more than a quarter century, these books were much prized by teenagers. I know from firsthand experience: I owned a stack of them.

"If the Holy Bible was printed as an Ace Double", editor Terry Carr once quipped, "it would be cut down to two 20,000-word halves with the Old Testament retitled as *Master of Chaos* and the New Testament as *The Thing With Three Souls*." It's easy to laugh at these books in hindsight, but they featured many of the leading genre writers of the 20th century, including Philip K. Dick, Isaac Asimov, Ursula K. Le Guin, Harlan Ellison, Robert Silverberg, Fritz Leiber, and Samuel R. Delany. By the way, many of these authors are now assigned in college classes, although in more sober editions, with the buxom heroines and creepy aliens left off the covers.

In *Gold and Iron*, Vance delivers on the essential elements that made these books so popular. His hero Roy Barch is cast from the same mold that would later give us Han Solo and Indiana Jones. (Indeed, when I picture our protagonist, I keep coming back to a young Harrison Ford.) He's an individualist and risk-taker, and continually surprises extraterrestrials by his take-charge attitude — or what the aliens call "the dynamic thrust of your race." Barch's plan is a simple one, but far too bold for even pulp fiction: he plans to defeat an entire technologically-advanced civilization by himself. Did I mention that he is unarmed and living in a cave? Okay, maybe he will get a little help from his friends too...but allies are in short supply in this war-of-the-worlds confrontation.

The best thing about Jack Vance's adventure stories are the many ways he subverts the formulas. If you read enough of his tales, you soon learn that good guys aren't always so good, and bad guys aren't always so bad. His heroes form coalitions, alliances change, and events take a life of their own — more like real life than what you typically find inside an Ace Double. That's true in *Gold and Iron*, just as in Vance's more famous titles, such as *Emphyrio* or *The Dragon Masters*. Even when you think you have grasped the "dynamic thrust" of the story, it will shift in an unexpected direction.

Here too readers are treated to Vance's other trademarks: the fanciful language, the diversity of cultural traits, the hero who can never quite accept the role of insider, but is equally incapable of remaining an outsider. I wonder how many of Vance's teenage fans picked up on these subtleties. Probably not many. But these are key reasons why his books have held up so well more than a half-century after they were written. Many writers can follow the recipe and dish out action according to accepted formulas. But Vance was one of the few who could live up to all the demands of genre fiction, yet also aim for something larger, more delicate or sophisticated.

So enjoy the action of *Gold and Iron*. There are plenty of explosions and surprise attacks here. But also linger over the jazz, the conversations, the wry observations on personalities and cultures, and the other 'extras' Vance tossed into the mix. If the basic premise of the Ace Double was that you got more for your buck (or, rather, one-third of a buck) than the competition delivered, Vance certainly lived up to that promise in these pages. With a story this good, you might even decide to double down and, instead of flipping the book over to the upside down text, go back and read it all over again.

— Ted Gioia

Ted Gioia writes on literature, music and popular culture. He is the author of ten books, and runs the sci-fi website *Conceptual Fiction*.

CHAPTER I

MARKEL, THE LEKTHWAN, occupied a strange and beautiful dwelling on the highest crag of Mount Whitney, consisting of six domes, three minarets, and a wide terrace. The domes were formed of almost clear crystal, the minarets were white porcelain-stuff, the surrounding terrace was blue glass, and in turn was surrounded by a rococo balustrade with blue and white spiral stanchions.

To Earther minds, Markel was like his dwelling — beautiful, incomprehensible, disturbing. His skin shone lustrous gold; his features were fine, hard, exotic in their spacing. He wore soft black garments: tight breeches, sandals resting on two inches of air, a cloak which fell into dramatic shapes apparently of its own volition.

Markel welcomed no strangers, made no appointments, but contrived to conduct a large volume of business with small effort. He employed a dozen agents, conferring daily with each via Lekthwan three-dimensional television, which produced the illusion of face-to-face discussion. He occasionally flew abroad in his air-boat, occasionally received visitors from other Lekthwan domes.

His two Earther attendants, Claude Darran and Roy Barch, found him formal, courteous, painfully patient. Some of their duties were familiar enough, with parallels from their own experience: washing down the terrace, polishing the air-boat; others involved apparently irrational operations. When they made mistakes, Markel repeated his instructions, while Darran and Barch reacted each to his temperament, Darran ruefully apologetic, Barch listening with grim concentration.

Markel's psychological attitude was perhaps as much due to preoccupation as any innate conviction of superiority. On occasion he extended himself to be gracious. Noticing a mark on Barch's chin, he asked, "How did you do that?"

"Cut myself shaving," said Barch.

Markel's eyebrows flickered in surprise. He entered the dome, returning a few minutes later with a flask of clear liquid. "Wipe this over your face and you'll never need to shave again."

Barch looked dubiously at the bottle. "I've heard of stuff like this. It takes your face along with the beard."

Markel shook his head politely. "You need not worry in this case." He turned away, then paused. "A ship will be arriving today; my family will be aboard. We will receive them formally at eleven o'clock. Is that clear?"

"Very well," said Barch.

"You understand the landing operation?"

"Perfectly," said Barch.

Markel nodded, continued around the terrace, the space under his sandals giving him a springing striding gait. Barch went to the quarters he shared with Darran, cautiously applied the depilatory to his face. When he felt his cheeks, the stubble had disappeared.

Darran came in. "There's going to be a shake-up. The old man's family is arriving today — a wife, two daughters. Now everybody toes the mark, Markel included."

Barch nodded. "I know. He asked me if I remembered how to fold down the balustrade. Also he said 'formal' — that means the monkey-suits." He glanced sourly at his skin-tight green coveralls with the blue jacket. "I feel like a ballet dancer in that outfit." He handed Darran the bottle. "Here, make yourself beautiful. It's depilatory, removes your beard — a present from Markel. If we had ten gallons, we'd be millionaires."

Darran weighed the flask in his hand. "Some kind of hint? Maybe we're looking seedy."

"If it was deodorant, I might think so."

Darran looked at his wrist-watch. "Ten-thirty; we'd better get into our uniforms."

When they arrived at the landing stage, Markel already stood by the balustrade. He inspected them briefly, then, pulling the peak-visored cap lower over his eyes, turned to look out over the panorama to the south.

Moments passed. Down from the sky floated a glistening ball, striped red, gold, blue and silver. It expanded swiftly, the stripes flashing and whirling. Barch and Darran bent over the balustrade, felt for the locks. The balustrade collapsed into the blue glass, and a blast of cold air blew across the terrace.

The space-ball loomed overhead like a mountain, the stripes boiling and melting like the colors of a soap bubble. It pressed close, locked to the terrace.

The hull broke open into an arched portal. Markel stood like a statue; Barch and Darran stared.

Five Lekthwans came forth: two women, two men, a little girl who ran gaily across the terrace. Markel cried out a greeting, lifted the child high with one golden arm, with the other embraced the two women. There were a few moments of staccato Lekthwan conversation; then Markel set down the child, led the party into the near rotunda.

From the portal slid a dozen crates, cushioned on two inches of air, like Markel's sandals. Barch and Darran guided them one at a time to the service dome.

The portal closed, the colors in the hull boiled furiously. The space-ball drifted back from the landing stage, spun off into the east.

Darran and Barch, left alone on the terrace, watched it dwindle to a spot of color.

"Well, that's that," said Darran. "Now we've seen the big shot's family." He waited, but Barch made no comment. They lifted the balustrade back into place. "The older woman must be his wife," Darran went on reflectively, "and the two girls, his daughters."

"Cute little kid," said Barch.

Darran turned him a quizzical glance. "How about the other one?"

Barch bent over a crate. "Why argue? She's beautiful." He glanced briefly toward the rotunda. "She's still something off another planet, strange as a fish."

"She looks nineteen or twenty," Darran said ruminatively. "Of course, with Lekthwans you can't tell. Maybe she's forty."

"What's the difference?"

"No difference."

Barch grinned. "At night all cats are gray, so the saying goes."

"Sure," said Darran. "After all, they are human. What did Shylock say? 'If you cut me I bleed' —"

Barch said gruffly, "Go recite to the Lekthwans; they need indoctrination, not me."

Darran shrugged. "We're making a good thing out of the Lekthwans. They pay through the nose for everything we sell them. They've advanced us hundreds of years. We're building spaceships with principles of science we never even dreamed of. We've cut the death-rate with their medicine —"

"It's not our science, nor our medicine."

"It works, doesn't it?"

"It never grew on Earth, it's not good transplanting that alien stuff."

Darran regarded him curiously. "If you don't like the Lekthwans, how come you're up here working for Markel?"

Barch turned him a speculative glance. "I could ask you the same question."

"I'm here because I might learn something."

Barch abruptly turned away. "Guys like you are too easy-going. You want to be nice."

"Sure. It's nice to be nice."

"Are the Lekthwans nice to you? Maybe they come down to visit your house, buy you a beer?" Barch snorted. "Not on your life. They're Lekthwans, we're the peasants."

"Give them time," said Darran. "They're a long way ahead, we're strangers to each other. They're decent enough — maybe a little stand-offish."

Barch's bright hazel eyes glittered like coals. "And in a few years — what then? We were doing pretty well as Earthers, making progress every year. Homegrown, native, natural progress. Do you know what's going to happen to us? In those few more years you talk about, we'll be through. We won't be any good as Lekthwans — they won't have us — and we'll be a hell of a lot worse as Earthers."

Darran gravely tapped Barch's chest. "I'll tell you something. You'll never win a prize for optimism."

"Show me something to be optimistic about," growled Barch. "I keep thinking of a picture I once saw, a Zulu chief in his best clothes. A plug hat, a swallow-tail coat and underneath — a grass belly-band. That's what we're getting from the Lekthwans: the plug hat and the old coat."

"You've got your opinion," said Darran, "I've got mine." He bent over a crate, gave it a shove toward the door. "Let's be realistic. The Lekthwans are here. We can't turn back the clock. Why should we want to? We've got a lot to gain."

"Only what they decide is good for us."

Darran shook his head. "Earthers at Lekthwan schools learn anything they want to."

"First you've got to know the language."

Darran laughed. "Do you expect them to run their schools in English?…I'd give a lot to go to their planet." Darran laughed cheerfully. "You're looking through the wrong end of the telescope. Maybe you ought to go to Lekthwa yourself. It might give you a different slant."

"If I go to Lekthwa, I'll go to learn something pretty basic, and that's how to ease these gold-plate snobs off of Earth."

CHAPTER II

TKZ MAERKL-ELAKSD — Markel, as the Earthers called him — awaiting his wife Tcher, his daughters Komeitk Lelianr and Sia Spedz, stood looking through the wall of his south salon across the great California deserts. He wore no cloak; afternoon sunlight coppered the gold of his skin.

Behind him sounded the quick pad of feet; Sia Spedz came running out barefoot, wearing a diaphane diaper with white pompons at each hip. Her hair was finest platinum floss, burnished and waxed, parted in the middle, flared playfully over the ears. She stood on tiptoe by the wall looking out over the view. "Where are the other domes? Are we all alone?"

Markel stroked her head. "No, there are agencies all around Earth."

"And always on the mountain tops?"

"Yes, that's how we secure isolation and privacy." He turned as his wife and his second daughter appeared, wearing simple white kirtles. Tcher, the mother, dressed her hair sleek as a silver cap against her head. Komeitk Lelianr, the daughter, combed hers into a high tuft, like a silver flame.

Markel brought forth couches of half-living white foam. "And your voyage, was it pleasant?"

Komeitk Lelianr grimaced. Tcher said, "Everywhere but at Great Dark Cloud. A Klau web forced us to stop."

Markel stirred uneasily in his seat. "And then?"

"A boat clamped alongside, intending to send aboard a search party."

"But why? Why?"

"We were not told. There is a rumor that a dozen Lenape escaped from Magarak and the Klau would not have them win back to Lenau."

"No, a great defeat for the Klau." For 'defeat' Markel used an untranslatable Lekthwan word conveying overtones of angry retreat, loss of face, diminution of moral vitality. Murmured Markel, "They become intolerable... And then?"

"The ship master behaved with enormous dignity. He commenced a sight and sound broadcast of the Klau anxiety, and in five minutes they withdrew."

Markel conveyed his understanding through the complex Lekthwan eyebrow, eye and eyelash mood-language, and by the same method indicated a change in subject. He turned to Sia Spedz: "Tell me, how goes your gain of life-experience?"

The girl wriggled her toes. "Everyone commends my ability. I have learned eleven characterizations and three optionals, which are: *Smiling Sunrise, Playful Kitten* and *The Solitary One.*"

"Excellent."

Tcher said with whimsical pride, "She can walk twenty feet high on her sandals, and she went alone out around Mirska-Moon in a dayboat."

"On Earth she must be more cautious," said Markel. "Lekthwans are not universally popular."

Sia Spedz asked in puzzlement, "Why is that? Do we not help them, do we not train them at our Lekthwan schools?"

Markel smiled quietly. "The Earthers have long considered themselves unique in the universe, and the coming of the Lekthwans has been a blow to their pride."

Sia Spedz continued doubtfully. "Also I know all the Lekthwan reigns, dynasties and realms, starting with King Phalder in the Proto-History."

"Down on the plains of Earth, you will find natives in roughly the same stage of culture."

"That is more to the interest of Lelianr."

Markel turned to his other daughter. "Time fleets like a meteor streak; I cannot believe that you have finished your first curricula. And now?"

Komeitk Lelianr spoke in the *Sedate Counsel* characterization. "I think in several directions. Primitive anthropology concerns me, and also food research. Last month I designed a very pleasant sugar, of which several tons were produced and distributed."

Markel laughed. "If you would discover new and exotic flavors, test some of the Earther food."

Komeitk Lelianr screwed her face into a wry grimace. "Animal tissues."

"They also consume much plant matter."

"Life devouring life, nevertheless."

"An intrinsic immorality which I believe goes unrecognized. However, the race can synthesize only the simplest carbohydrates."

"I suppose they must feed themselves somehow."

"The Earthers are not entirely savage; indeed, if you pursue your interest in proto-culture you will come upon some surprising achievements."

Komeitk Lelianr nodded. "I have also considered a career in the creation of art-spectacles."

"Last month," said Tcher, "she completed a beautiful work in the Empire style, which won commendation in the Arianum."

Markel's characterization indicated doubt. "It is a career with potentialities for great fulfillment or equally intense disappointment."

"Depending on the creator's vitality and largeness of spirit."

"Perhaps you are so gifted. However I hate to see you chancing the composure and happiness of your life."

Komeitk Lelianr assumed a characterization of whimsical recklessness. "Success is the same in any field, and failure is failure."

"You would be most secure in food research. Primitive anthropology drains the emotion, especially if one fails to control his empathy."

Komeitk Lelianr shrugged. "There is still time for me to decide, and I need not limit myself to rigid specialization."

Sia Spedz cried, "Look, two Earthers on the terrace!"

Markel changed his characterization. "They are my servants — both bright young men."

"They are not quite as I had pictured Earthers," Komeitk Lelianr remarked thoughtfully.

Tcher said, "The darker of the two seems more agreeable, the other has weight on his soul."

"As a matter of fact," said Markel, "Roy has little liking for the Lekthwans."

Tcher shook her head. "If the Klau had come to Earth in our place, then he would have grounds for resentment."

"He has grounds, of a rather personal nature. His father was a scientist, and Roy's ambition was to follow in his father's footsteps. From earliest youth he trained himself in the accepted techniques. Then the Lekthwans came, and overnight the entire effort of his life became nothing. Much of what he had learned was inaccurate, the remainder in the light of Lekthwan knowledge was either obsolete or rudimentary. Roy became very bitter."

Komeitk Lelianr studied Barch's back. "Understandably."

"Why does he not study on Lekthwa?" demanded Sia Spedz.

Markel considered Barch and Darran. "He may approach the idea. At the moment all he sees is long years of further study, where he must start learning with children the age of Spedz."

"The other," said Tcher, "indeed has a much kinder expression. What is his name?"

"That is Claude. He is more practical than Roy, and on the whole, less emotional. I plan to include him in the next group to Lekthwa."

"And Roy?"

"So far he has shown no inclination to leave Earth."

Markel's two guests entered the salon. He rose to his feet. "You have refreshed yourselves?"

"We have bathed and rested. The view from your dome is magnificent."

Markel nodded. "I consider Earth among the more beautiful worlds. Have you noticed the valley to the southeast, the hundred soft colors?"

"Beautiful."

"Beautiful, and also deadly. Indeed the Earthers call it 'Death Valley'."

Chapter III

Barch and Darran cooked for themselves, with supplies delivered every Saturday by helicopter. By and large their duties were nominal, and after washing down the terrace, their mornings were free. During this time Darran studied the Lekthwan grammar texts and tape recordings that Markel had placed at his disposal, while Barch read or moodily sunned himself.

The arrival of Markel's family disturbed the routine. On the morning after her arrival, Sia Spedz made friends with Darran, asking him why he wore shoes, rather than air-sandals.

Darran's answer was completely honest. "In the first place, I own no air-sandals. In the second, I'd fall flat on my face if I tried them."

"But it's not hard," said Sia Spedz, speaking English with a precise accent, "so long as you stay close to the ground."

"How high can a person walk?"

Sia Spedz looked into the sky. "A man could walk up to the moon, if he were skillful enough. I can walk twenty feet from the ground."

"I don't understand. Why should it be easier close to the ground?"

"The force comes out like a pyramid. Close to the ground the base is broad. The higher you walk, the narrower becomes the column you walk on, so much the harder to balance."

"Ah," said Darran. "Why don't you make more powerful sandals, so that even when you walk high there would be a wide pyramid under your feet?"

"I don't know...I think because then there would be no fun in learning."

"I thought you were a practical race," said Darran.

"Not entirely. The Klau are completely practical. Everything is planned for exact use, whether it makes people happy or not. There is no gaiety on the Klau worlds."

"So? Who are the Klau?"

"Enemies. Terrible men, with eyes like red stars." But Sia Spedz was more interested in her skill with the sandals. "Watch." She climbed into the air as if she were mounting stairs, ran gaily back and forth over Darran's head. "Now I'm going higher."

"Be careful!" Darran walked back and forth below her with arms outstretched.

"This is as high as I like to go," said Sia Spedz. "Up here it's very shaky."

"You'd better come down. You make me nervous."

She rejoined him. "Why don't you ask Markel to give you a pair of sandals?"

Darran shrugged. "It's not polite to ask for gifts."

"If you don't make your wants known, they go unrecognized."

Darran laughed. "I thought you weren't a practical race."

"Perhaps we are after all. In any event I'll give you a pair of sandals myself."

"You'll get spanked for giving away your father's best shoes."

Sia Spedz giggled. "That's a funny thing to say."

Barch had been leaning on the balustrade. "I think he's funny too. He knows all kinds of games. Get him to teach you hopscotch."

"Hopscotch?" Sia Spedz looked at Darran. "What is that?"

"It's a game little Earth girls play."

"Do you know how to play?"

Darran scratched his cheek. "Roy plays a lot better than I do."

"No," said Barch, "you won yesterday."

"You show me, Claude."

Barch sat down on a bench. "I'll see that there's no cheating." He reached under him, pulled out Darran's Lekthwan Primer. He flipped it open, and glanced at the introduction.

"The Lekthwan language," read the book, "sounds harsh and consonantal to Earth ears — a matter which perhaps deserves explanation. To begin with, the Lekthwan language embraces a tremendous vocabulary, with sometimes a hundred synonyms for one basic idea. In consequence there is no need for circumlocution, and Lekthwan speech is notable for the logical simplicity of its declarative forms.

"This characteristic has led, in the evolution of the language, to the extensive use of contractions and abbreviations, resulting in a preponderance of consonant sounds.

"A further peculiarity of the Lekthwan language is the fact that each word may have a number of different shadings, depending upon the 'characterization' assumed by the person speaking, or even the person spoken to. There are almost a hundred of these characterizations, of which sixty-two are termed *basic*. Every mature person is familiar with the basic characterizations, and with most of the remaining optionals. The Lekthwan indicates the characterization in which he speaks by play of eyes, eyebrows and eyelashes. In crude analogy the characterizations might be likened to the emotion-masks of the ancient Greek dramatists.

"It is evident from the above that the Lekthwan language is exquisitely subtle, flexible and difficult of mastery. This present course, therefore, is designed to acquaint the student with Lekthwan-basic, with an elementary vocabulary from the most literal and least fanciful of the characterizations, i.e.: No. 2, the so-called *Statistician*."

Barch tossed the book back to the bench, mentally labeling the Lekthwan language a life-time job in itself...The Lekthwan children seemed to absorb it easily enough. He watched Sia Spedz, engrossed in Darran's explanation. How many of these characterizations was she able to use? A bright-looking kid. Thousands of years of natural — and possibly eugenic — selection had no doubt increased the intelligence of the race. Intelligence and — as if to offer an illustration, Komeitk Lelianr stepped out on the terrace — intelligence and beauty.

Covertly he watched her as she leaned upon the balustrade. The Lekthwans, he knew, felt no self-consciousness in connection with nudity. Komeitk Lelianr now wore only a short skirt and air-sandals. Barch felt the warmth rising in his body. A stranger, a creature of a far world...Still how wonderful, how alive, how graceful, how clean...

She turned quickly, as if she had felt his eyes. Barch looked away guiltily, then after a moment glanced back, to where she now stood with her back to the balustrade.

She was appraising him. Barch thought bitterly, I'm the first Earther savage she's had a close look at.

She said politely, "I see that you study our language. Do you find it difficult?"

She meant to be pleasant, thought Barch. The college girl interviewing the Zulu buck. Being nice. Barch rose to his feet. "I don't find it difficult because I'm not working at it."

She said nothing, gazing at him with embarrassing intensity.

Barch said, "At first glance it looks complicated. I imagine that it's a remarkable vehicle of expression, if a stranger could ever digest it."

Her face showed interest. Barch thought angrily, she probably expected me to grunt like a bear.

Komeitk Lelianr inquired, "Aren't you the one who doesn't like us?"

Barch's eyes narrowed in surprise. He said carefully, "I don't object to Lekthwans as human beings."

"And that's all you feel?"

"I don't think that Earth will ultimately benefit from their presence."

Komeitk Lelianr asked, "What's your name?"

"Roy Barch." And almost rudely, he asked, "What's yours?"

"Komeitk Lelianr."

"Mmph…What does it mean?"

She laughed. "A meaning? Why should it have a meaning?"

"It seems reasonable that an advanced people — as you profess yourselves to be — would use your names for indices, to indicate your profession, or home, or some kind of identification."

"Tsk," said Komeitk Lelianr. Her eyebrows moved in what Barch recognized as a change of characterization. "What a terrible idea: regimented, uniform. You suffer misapprehensions about us."

"No less than your misapprehensions about us," growled Barch.

Komeitk Lelianr grinned. "Does your name mean anything?"

"No."

"I'd like to ask a favor of you," she said.

"You don't need to ask favors. I'm on the payroll; all you need to do is give orders."

"I'm very much interested in the psychology of other-world races. Would you object if I made a psychometric test of you?"

"Ah," said Barch bitterly. "So now it comes out. I'm to figure as one of your case-histories…Typical Zulu buck. Perhaps you'd like a photograph of me in my war-bonnet? Or maybe recording me in my native chants?"

"That would be wonderful," said Komeitk Lelianr. "But — do you have your regalia here?"

Barch stared at her. She was unquestionably serious. "We're going to throw a combination cannibal-feed and voodoo orgy tomorrow night on Sunset Boulevard. If you sneak quietly over in your air-sandals, you'll get some really sensational stuff."

Her eyebrows flickered in interest. "Indeed, I would like to visit one of these rites."

"Well," said Barch thoughtfully, "you'd have to disguise yourself. If you powdered over your skin, you probably could pass for a good case of sun-tan…Also you'd have to wear a few more clothes. That's a provocative outfit you've got on now."

"I'm not sure I understand. Why do you say that?"

Barch looked away. "I don't know…Yes, I do too."

"Then how should I dress myself?"

He looked sidewise at her. "Are you serious?"

"Of course. Where is this Sunset Boulevard?"

"I could take you," said Barch thoughtfully.

"That would be very helpful."

Barch calculated. "How will we get there?"

"In the air-boat. How else?"

"Your father won't kick?"

"Kick?"

"Object?"

"Of course not." She added soberly, "You must understand, I possibly intend to make anthropology my career."

Barch nodded. "Very well, that's a date."

"But what sort of costume must I wear?"

"Anything that covers you from shoulder to knee. If you combed your hair back I suppose you could pass for platinum blonde…"

CHAPTER IV

DARRAN CAME IN while Barch was knotting his tie. "Where do you think you're going? Why the preparations?"

"Got a date with the old man's daughter."

Darran sat down. "So? Hopscotch with Spedz maybe, along the north terrace?"

"No, sir. Catch-as-catch-can with the cute one, up to San Francisco."

Darran leaned back limply. "This is fantastic."

"Not when you get the background. She's interested in picturesque native customs; she thinks she's going to Los Angeles to see a human sacrifice, or a Dionysian fertility rite."

Darran sighed. "What some guys won't do to get a date... And where are you taking her? Or is she taking you?"

"Darned if I know. She'd probably enjoy the Embarcadero saloons or Chutes at the Beach." He made a wry face. "I have my pride too."

"She'd be bored at the Fairmont."

"I should think so. No blood-letting, no colorful rituals."

"There's always Hambone Kelly's."

"True," said Barch. "There's always Hambone Kelly's." He buttoned his jacket. "Well, here I go."

"Good luck," said Darran. "Don't get in trouble."

Barch turned him a cool stare. "What do you mean by that?"

"Nothing," said Darran mildly. "You're a truculent son of a gun... You must have something on your mind."

Barch pushed out upon the terrace and stood looking into the night. His hands were clammy and tense; Darran had hit close to the truth. This was like going out on the first date of his life, only more so.

He walked slowly around the terrace, stopped near the main dome. Inside were Lekthwans, from a far planet; did they expect him to knock on the door, call for the girl? Or should he wait outside until she appeared? He made an angry sound through his teeth; where was his self-respect? He was as good as any of them; this was Earth, by God, they'd go by Earth customs.

He strode belligerently up to the dome, then came to a halt. Knock, certainly. Or ring a bell. But where?

Light glimmered through the opacity; Barch backed away. Komeitk Lelianr came quickly out upon the terrace, followed by Markel and Sia Spedz running like a terrier.

Markel spoke in Lekthwan. "I imagine you'll be disappointed…Of course there's no reason why you shouldn't investigate."

Sia Spedz said, "I'd like to go too."

"One anthropologist in the family is enough," said Markel. He turned to Barch. "See that she does nothing to get into trouble, Roy."

"Tsk." Komeitk Lelianr sauntered down the terrace. "Come, Roy."

Barch, mustering his dignity, followed to where the air-boat floated.

Komeitk Lelianr ducked into the air-boat, Barch followed. She wore a white and black one-piece suit, like a harlequin costume. She would be conspicuous, but would not necessarily draw a crowd.

Inside the boat floated a silver ball pierced by a black rod. Komeitk Lelianr took the ball; the car moved off into the sky. "Now," she said, "which way?"

The first thing, thought Barch, was to get the affair on its proper footing. "Show me how to run this contraption."

She turned her head, her eyebrows raised in surprise. For a moment Barch thought she might politely ignore him; then she handed him the silver ball. "This —" she touched the black rod "— represents the perpendicular axis of the boat. Tilt the ball, the boat tilts. Move the ball up, you initiate a cumulative upward acceleration, which can only be countered by moving the ball down. The black rod is the speed control. The farther you depress it, the faster you go. To brake, you push from below."

"That's simple enough…Where's the height indicator?"

"There." She pointed to a series of angular black shapes moving along a pale gray band. "This is at once the altimeter and the speed indicator.

The green circle in the middle represents the boat. The outline of the shadows depicts the profile of the land directly ahead. The lower you fly, the larger becomes the green circle. The green touches the black when the boat touches ground."

Barch nodded. "It seems easy enough."

She watched intently for a moment or two, then asked, "Where are you heading?"

"San Francisco Bay, four hundred miles north."

"Markel tells me," she said, "that the Earthers have not been cannibals for a number of years. Why did you inform me otherwise?"

"Ha, ha," said Barch. "You failed to identify my characterization."

Komeitk Lelianr pursed her lips. "I had no idea that the Earthers employed characterizations."

"Not formally."

"And this characterization — what do you call it?"

"The *Sarcastic Zulu*."

"Odd."

"Very."

"What then is the rite to which you are taking me?"

"It's called 'an evening out with a pretty girl'."

"Oh?"

"We're going to a place called Hambone Kelly's across the bay from San Francisco…Or would you prefer a more decorous approach to Earth nightlife?"

"I suppose I must rely upon your judgment as to what might interest me."

"I don't know much about your frame of mind…Tell me something, how old are you?"

"Fifty-two." At Barch's surprised glance, she explained. "That would be twenty of your years."

"Your name is hard to pronounce," said Barch. "I'll call you 'Ellen'."

In the dark he could not see the expression of her face. "Whatever is convenient for you." She reached, drew out a shelf, on which a chart was outlined in faintly glowing lines.

In the soft light Barch noticed that while she had dulled her skin to soft tan, her lips, untouched, glittered like gold-leaf.

"There's something that must be done," said Barch. "I hate to do it."

"What's that?"

"Lipstick. Hideous stuff that Earth girls smear on their mouths. But it's got to be done."

A lonesome cluster of lights appeared below, a luminous flower on a dark pasture. Barch gingerly lowered the boat, the lights spread apart. On the altimeter band the green circle grew wider, while the black shadow representing the terrain stretched lengthwise. The green and black met; the boat landed in a field opposite the town. Komeitk Lelianr watched him patiently.

"Would you like to get out?" Barch asked politely.

She hesitated. "Why?"

"No reason at all," said Barch. "Sit still."

She pushed through the hull, stood beside him in the darkness. A warm wind brought the smell of dust and dry hay. From a tent not far distant came a scuffling roar and a blare of music. "Roller-skating rink," said Barch briefly. "We go this way."

"Where?"

"Over to that little drugstore. I'll buy you some lipstick."

He reached out, took her hand. Her fingers went tense, then relaxed limply. In the red, green, yellow lights from the roller rink, Barch noticed a fastidious set to her mouth.

They crossed the highway. "You'd better wait out here," said Barch. "I'll only be a minute."

She stood in the shadows, a white and black harlequin shape, hair glinting in the colored lights. Barch, looking over his shoulder, thought nothing had ever hit him like this, coming and going; repulsion, attraction.

When he returned, she was nowhere in sight. "Ellen! Ellen!" A pair of young bucks in faded jeans and sport shirts looked at him curiously.

He saw her by the roller rink, watching the swirling shapes inside. He walked to where she stood. "You gave me a scare."

She looked up with brief curiosity.

Barch said crossly. "I'm more or less responsible for you."

She looked back into the rink. "You need not feel so." Barch wondered in what characterization she spoke.

She nodded toward the dusty floor. "On the planet Eifal, they skate somewhat similarly on ice, and also on Pterni, although there they use electric skates and move like lightning."

"We skate on ice here too." His voice hung lamely in the air. She made no response.

After a moment he asked. "How many planets have you visited?"

"Oh — ten or twelve."

Barch felt illogically angry. "I suppose you check on native customs wherever you go?"

"I became interested in anthropology when we visited the anthropological museum on Baliberos. The Savants have tended it since the beginning of Baliberos' history."

"Not as primitive as the Earthers, then?"

She considered. "No, I would say not. A very much older race, of course, with a remarkable architectural technique."

Barch watched the skaters with unseeing eyes. This wouldn't work out. In his mind a scathing voice asked, what wouldn't work out? Barch evaded the question. It was easier to be angry. The college girl and the Zulu guide... Damn it, he told himself fiercely, I'll make it work out! I'm human and she's human. I don't care if she's visited a thousand planets...

He turned determinedly back to her, took her hand, led her to where a patch of garish light poured from a window. "Stand still, and I'll put on your lipstick for you."

"Let me see it." She examined the metal case, the red paste. "What is it?"

"Aniline dye, wax, perfume. Perfectly harmless... Hold up your face." She looked up into his eyes a foot away.

The pulse in his throat nearly choked him.

He lifted up the lipstick.

He paused, swallowing hard. She looked up at him.

He clenched an arm around her; her waist was supple as silk; he kissed the surprised golden mouth, tenderly.

She drew back, wiped at her face. "Why did you do that?"

Barch said huskily, "Do you want the real news?"

"Of course."

"That's a sign of passion. Some call it love."

"Oh…I suppose it's to be expected. But don't do it again; it's not sanitary."

Barch's head was still whirling. Anger or fright would have stimulated him; he would have kissed her again. "Sanitation be damned… Here…" He put his hand behind her head, daubed lipstick on her mouth. "That's good enough."

In silence they returned across the field to the boat. Barch grasped the ball; the boat rose into the night.

Barch said presently, "Do you know what I mean by the word 'love'?"

"I suppose so. It has a different aspect in each of our characterizations; I imagine Earth love is included somewhere among them."

"Tell me," Barch said earnestly, "could you ever love me?"

She studied him with startled amusement, and seemed to inch slightly away. "Are Earthers usually so abrupt?"

Barch said through clenched teeth, "I talk too much. I make a fool of myself. Forget it."

"We Lekthwans are a peculiar race," said Komeitk Lelianr kindly. "Try to think of us as impersonal beings."

"Same way with the Earthers," muttered Barch. "Think of us as impersonal beings."

Chapter V

Hills brought angular shapes to the altimeter band. A long carpet of light spread out below: San Leandro, Oakland, Berkeley. Barch flew a thousand feet over the shore of the bay, slanted down over San Pablo Avenue. "I think there's a vacant lot where we can leave the boat. Yes, there."

He set the car down behind a row of eucalyptus trees. "Now we start."

From Hambone Kelly's, music came loud and strong to the street. "Another roller rink?" asked Komeitk Lelianr.

Barch was feeling dull and dead. "No. People come here to dance and drink and listen to music."

"Interesting! Interpretive dancing, I suppose, with sexual symbolism?"

"Well, I don't know about that. It's energetic dancing, at least."

"And what do you mean, 'drink'?"

"People take stimulating drinks to heighten their awareness, so that they enjoy themselves more intensely."

"Oh... And the music?"

Barch was warming to the subject. "I brought you purposely to hear the music — a special kind of music that may be new to you."

She listened. "Eight-part polyphony, is it not?"

Barch started at her. "There's only seven pieces in the band."

"There's one — a tinkling kind of harp that's playing in two parts."

"Oh, the piano." Barch was feeling worse now. "Let's go in."

He led her to a dim table. On a raised stage stood seven men playing trumpet, trombone, clarinet, piano, drums, banjo, and brass bass.

They played with brilliant emphasis; music poured forth clear and impelling.

Barch said close to Komeitk Lelianr's ear, "This is the Yerba Buena Jazz Band. They're playing a tune called *Weary Blues.*"

"It sounds not at all weary."

"No, quite the reverse." Barch turned to watch the band.

Music came in a tide, the trumpet ringing like a bar of pure energy; the trombone dark, rough, hoarse; the clarinet a fiery bird. There came the final chatter and smash of traps, then the sigh of release from the audience, deep from the stomach, the chest, the throat.

Barch turned to Komeitk Lelianr. "What do you think of it?"

"It seems loud and emotional."

"It's the music of our times," said Barch fervently. "It reflects our racial drive; it's the best of our contemporary creativeness."

Komeitk Lelianr leaned forward. "You appear to think in symbolic images," she remarked. "Am I right?"

"I don't know," replied Barch impatiently. "It's not important; won't you forget primitive anthropology for awhile?"

Barch saw her eyebrows flicker. "You do it automatically," he said bitterly.

"What?"

"Jump into characterizations. Find whatever role works out best at the moment, then get into it."

She frowned. "I've never thought of it in quite that way."

He made an impatient gesture. "Forget it...Tell me, what kind of music do the Lekthwans listen to?"

"Our music is much different from this. It's hard to explain. There is first the *Liddrsk* mode — an underlying base or legato, with notes falling on it like rain; then there is the *Cmodor*, in which a group of notes start in the distance, approach, certain notes advancing, then falling back, and all meeting at a core. Then there is the *Lyzg* mode — but it's even more complicated."

She turned her head to watch the dancing. "On Jeol last year we witnessed the Fuolghan — a religious ceremony with dancing much like this. It took place along the Sky-level, of course. And the music was different — the sound of metal wheels, and gongs of frozen hydrogen."

"Yes, yes," said Barch impatiently. "Music. That's why I brought you here. Listen."

Komeitk Lelianr listened. "Very interesting. But it jars me. It's too forthright, too uncompromising."

"No, no," cried Barch, with no very clear idea of what proposition he was contradicting. He spoke on with great intensity, willing that he arouse in her a feeling for the music and by extension, himself. "By your time-scale, we're a young people. Your own world is quiet, your people are settled, complacent. Earth is different! This is an exciting time for Earth — the more so since the coming of the Lekthwans. Every day is new, fresh; every day sees something started, progress made toward a goal…We live with this drive, this thrust to the future — a dynamism that speaks in music."

He waited but Komeitk Lelianr said nothing. Her thoughts were unreadable.

Barch qualified. "I should say, the spirit of our section of the world. On other continents people live differently, and their music is different. The Chinese consider all our music marching music — jazz, chamber music, hymns, dirges, all of it."

A waitress approached. "Order, please?"

"Tom Collins, a pair," said Barch. He said to Komeitk Lelianr, "But we are the dominant force, the leaders —" he compressed his mouth "— until the Lekthwans came."

She laughed. "You forgot that for a few moments."

"Yes. So I did."

"Why do you tell me all this?"

Barch hesitated, then took the plunge. "Because I don't consider myself a barbarian. I'm your equal, whether you like it or not. And —"

The waitress placed a pair of tall glasses in front of them. "Dollar twenty, please."

Barch dropped money on the tray.

"And?"

Barch hesitated, seeking the meaningful words. "There are a lot of prizes in this universe. A person has to fight for them. You're one of these prizes."

"Me?" Komeitk Lelianr laughed.

"Yes, you," said Barch doggedly. "I've got to make you know I realize it, and that I'm in the competition."

Komeitk Lelianr touched the glass, smelled of it gingerly. "What is this?"

"Fruit-juice, carbonated water, ethyl alcohol, sugar."

"Living matter?"

"What if it is?" snapped Barch. "Basically, it's carbon, oxygen, hydrogen; what difference does it make where it came from? The fruit is dead now."

She screwed up her face, sipped. "It's not unpleasant... Are these glasses sterile?"

"Probably not. That's why they put the alcohol in — to sterilize the glasses."

"Oh." After a moment she said, "What you say is interesting. Naturally I'm surprised at your ambitions."

"Naturally?" He accented the word.

"Why not? You saw me for the first time yesterday."

On her face Barch thought to detect a half-smile; the quick thought came that, no matter what color, what race, what stage of culture, feminine psychology remained the same. He saw her hand on the table, slim fingers absently touched the frosted glass. Barch's heart thudded under his shirt. He reached out, took her hand in his.

She frowned slightly, withdrew her hand. And under the table Barch saw the motion where she rubbed it against her black and white garment.

They sat in silence. The band returned to the stand. Komeitk Lelianr watched them a moment. She said quietly, "You feel no tenderness toward me, no sympathy; we have no hopes in common; we have not dealt together with hardship or disappointment. You may feel passion, but you feel no love."

Barch leaned forward, but his tongue found no words.

"You are not interested in me as a person." She continued stonily. "I'm no more than a symbol to you. I'm the 'richest prize' that your vanity tells you that you deserve."

Barch felt sudden shame. He felt his cheeks burn. He turned away, watched the band.

Music. Barch gripped the glass until his knuckles showed white. He felt Komeitk Lelianr's dispassionate observation, then an equally dispassionate study of the dancers. Barch, he told himself, you're the biggest damn fool the world has yet seen. From the corner of his eye he studied the girl's profile — clean-cut, delicate, proud. Barch, he said, the girl's too good for you. Not because she's a Lekthwan, but because you're a thick-headed boor...

He set his shoulders, somewhere found his voice. It sounded rough and strained to his ears. "I'm sorry I brought you out under false pretenses."

She said wistfully, "Then there really are none of the ceremonies you described?"

"Perhaps in the middle of Africa."

"One of the remoter districts?"

"Yes, quite remote," said Barch sardonically. "A different race of people entirely, as different from us as —" He was about to add, "as we are from you," then stopped short. He drank from the tall green glass.

He pointed to a negro sitting at a table nearby. "That man is of African stock."

"Oh? He seems no different from you except in skin coloring. Does he practice the ceremonies you speak of?"

"No, of course not. He's been born into our society. He does, however, sometimes run into unpleasant discrimination." And he added maliciously, "Much, I suspect, as Earthers on Lekthwa experience."

Komeitk Lelianr pursed her lips, turned the tall glass between her fingers. The film was wearing off, her golden skin glinted underneath. Barch noticed that she had barely tasted the drink. "Don't you like it?"

She looked down indifferently, sipped at the straws. "Should I now feel exhilarated?"

"Not unless you drink two or three more."

She shook her head. "That's not likely." She rose to her feet. "Now we will go."

Sullenly Barch followed her out to the street, and back to the airboat. Fighting to keep control of his voice he said, "If you are interested in sordid spectacles, I could take you to a prize fight or a wrestling match — although I'd prefer not."

She looked at him reflectively. "It would embarrass you?"

"Yes. It would embarrass me."

She shrugged. "Completely unnecessary; I am interested in Earth customs only from a scientific viewpoint. Perhaps you misunderstood my motives in arranging this trip."

Barch twisted his face in a wide humorless grin. "I don't think so. But it happens that I'm not interested in primitive rites myself, and my gallantry — or subservience — doesn't extend quite that far."

"Then we will return to the dome." She stepped through the hull, into the air-boat.

Chapter VI

The boat rose into the night, automatically turned back toward Markel's dome, far to the south. San Pablo Avenue became a bright artery, flowing with twinkling head-light corpuscles. Overhead, the sky was luminous, dusted with glow from a million lights.

The boat flew south across the great central valley. The cities became blurs of light astern; the sky was dark and bright with stars. Komeitk Lelianr leaned back into the cushions, looking up at the sky.

Barch sat stiffly, watching the towns and villages appearing ahead, fading to the rear. He had nothing to say; he had gone out to joust at windmills, he had been unhorsed, humiliated. In the aftermath, he could understand something of the situation's inevitability. But it would have been worse, he thought with gloomy satisfaction, if he had not asserted his right to try.

Komeitk Lelianr said softly, "I can see my native sun, up by that bright star…"

"That's Spica."

"Up and to the left is a fainter star — Skyl, our sun."

Barch contemplated the star without interest. "You sound as if you're homesick."

She nodded. "It's very lonely on a strange planet with none of my friends; therefore I seek to bury myself in study."

Barch lapsed into silence. Dark shadows on the altimeter showed rounded swellings, then ahead angular ridges.

Suddenly, low ahead, an intense green flash appeared in the sky. Komeitk Lelianr jerked up in her seat. She bent her head over a mesh, spoke staccato Lekthwan words.

There was no reply. A faint sound came from her throat.

Barch sat up. "What's the matter?"

"I don't know..." She drove home the speed button.

Shadows fled across the altimeter band. Komeitk Lelianr sat tense, clutching her knees; Barch looked uneasily ahead. Snowy peaks gleamed below; a few moments later Markel's dome appeared, faintly luminescent, peaceful.

The air-boat slowed, dropped, settled into its bay.

Komeitk Lelianr stepped quickly out. Barch followed. On the terrace she froze into a statue. Barch asked anxiously, "What's the trouble?"

"I don't know. I feel something — bad."

Barch started around the dark terrace. Fibers of green light glowed in the blue glass under his feet.

Ahead lay something dark. Barch ran forward, the muscles of his throat tight and stiff. He knelt slowly. Claude Darran. Barch stared in astonishment. Cold, dead — unthinkable!

A shape stood behind him: Komeitk Lelianr. Barch rose numbly to his feet. He walked forward; two paces, four — another dark shape. It was small, sprawled carelessly. Behind him he heard horrified gasping sounds. Barch's neck was cold as ice. He bent beside the pitiful object that had been Sia Spedz, then rising quickly, drew Komeitk Lelianr to the balustrade.

She said in an agonized whisper, "The Klau — they have come to Earth... They have been here..."

Barch peered into the darkness, feeling ineffectual, indecisive. He had no real desire to investigate, to confront a set of off-world murderers. From inside the dome came a sudden thud. Komeitk Lelianr whimpered, jerked forward.

Spasmodic strength came to Barch's legs; he shoved ahead of her, moved toward the dim-glowing portal. Cautiously he looked within: nothing but an article or two of furniture. Komeitk Lelianr pressed against his back breathing in soft sobs. He ducked inside; Komeitk Lelianr ran ahead, thrust aside a portiere of green smoke. She froze, arms and legs at grotesque angles.

Barch looked over her shoulder, down at two golden bodies. There was a great deal of blood, puddled and netted along the floor. Barch drew the dazed girl back.

She said, "I must communicate…" She walked awkwardly across the room, waved open a portal. Two more corpses — Markel's guests. And at the communication table sat a great black creature. Stiff black bristles framed his face; his eyes gleamed like polished jet, with red four-pronged centers.

The Klau stared at Barch; Barch's legs were numb, wooden. Grumbling, mumbling, the Klau arose, clutching a heavy black dagger.

Barch backed sweating against the wall; the Klau hacked. Barch caught the black wrist, planted a foot in the belly, kicked. The Klau lurched, toppled, fell with a dull roar of rage.

Barch, grinning like a wolf, planted his foot in the pulpy neck. Thick hands seized his ankle; Barch swayed.

He heard a hiss, a grunt. The hands clenched, the four-pronged red stars widened, slowly folded in on themselves.

Komeitk Lelianr arose from the dagger in the black chest.

"Come, we must go," she panted. "There are others!" Barch pointed questioningly to the communication table. "No — he has destroyed it."

She ran to the portal. Barch paused to wrench at the dagger. He heard a thin scream, looked up, saw a flurrying black shape. Something heavy, furry, enveloped him. His legs were swept out from under him, he was carried off like a swaddled child.

Hands gripped him hard, heaved. He was free, falling, falling — a hundred feet, a thousand feet, mile after mile…

Kicking frantically, Barch freed himself from the fur robe… Still falling… Strange there was no rush of wind, no pound or flutter at his arms and legs. He stiffened to rigidity. The air was calm. He was suspended, he floated in darkness, lack of gravity gave the illusion of free fall. Now his eyes adapted themselves, he could see walls glowing with a dull maroon light, as if red-hot. But the air was cold, there was no heat on his face.

Komeitk Lelianr floated quietly over his head. He caught an ankle, drew her down. Her eyes were closed.

Barch relaxed like a spent swimmer. Events were moving too fast.

He wondered, am I awake or asleep? This is too fantastic for reality. He tried to rouse himself, without success. I am already awake, he decided.

Inspecting the surroundings, he saw that they floated in an ovular cell with no apparent entrance. He felt, as much as heard, a high-pitched whine, so shrill as to be nearly inaudible.

He looked back to Komeitk Lelianr, touched her forehead. It felt hot and dry... A surge of pity made his eyes heavy; mother, father, sister — hacked, bloody, dead. A terrible sight. And why had they been spared? Why did they float in a cell?

Barch closed his eyes. He wanted to sleep, forget, ignore... He felt a stirring beside him. Komeitk Lelianr opened her eyes. She was completely matter-of-fact. She felt her head, licked her lips, looked around. Her eyes rested dispassionately on Barch.

Barch steadied his voice. "Well?"

"We're in a Klau ship."

"Where are they taking us? Why haven't they killed us?"

Komeitk Lelianr shrugged. "Corpses are valueless. We probably will end up at Magarak..."

"Magarak?"

"A manufacturing center."

"But —"

"We're slaves."

"Oh." Before Barch's eyes flashed the scenes of Earth like color slides. All this he was leaving. All this he would see no more. In a strained voice he said, "And what is this Magarak like?"

"Gray. Dank. Cold."

Barch felt a spasm of rage — toward Komeitk Lelianr, toward the Lekthwans. Why should he suffer in their quarrel? "Why don't the Lekthwans do something about these Klau?"

Komeitk Lelianr smiled half-contemptuously. "There are three Lekthwan planets, forty-two Klau worlds. There is war between us that perhaps you cannot completely understand — a long-range combat of our —" she sought for a word to express a complex Lekthwan idea "— moral vitality. In the end we will win. Meanwhile many people suffer." She shrugged. "The universe is not a paradise."

"No," said Barch. Earth suddenly seemed very small and negligible,

a bucolic backwater off to one side of the space-empires. "So then —
we spend the rest of our lives on Magarak?"

She made no answer. Barch glanced desperately around the glowing
walls. "Can't we be ransomed, can't we escape?"

She spoke slowly, as if to a child. "Ransom is inapplicable; there is
no medium of exchange between Lekthwa and the Klau. The Klau have
energy, raw material, technical skill. Labor is the scarcest commodity
of the universe; labor is the Klau wealth."

"And escape?"

She shrugged. "Recently a dozen Lenape hid in a false cargo blister,
and reached the Maha Triad. If they find a way home to Lenau, the
Klau will suffer. If they are recaptured — the Klau will use them to dis-
courage others."

"The main difficulty seems to be in leaving the planet."

"Exactly." She reached in a pouch at her belt, brought out an atomizer. Carefully she sprayed her face, her arms.

Barch watched her. "Why do you do that?"

"I think the Klau consider me an Earther. I would prefer it so…Give
me the lip-dye, please."

CHAPTER VII

TIME PASSED, PERHAPS TWO DAYS. Three times the walls swelled into blisters, bursting with a pop to eject packets of gray mush into the cell.

Komeitk Lelianr had completely withdrawn into herself. She spoke no words to Barch, ignored the food. Finally Barch pushed himself across to her. "If you don't eat, you'll be weak … You'll get sick."

She looked at him languidly. "What then?"

Barch truculently knit his brows. "What's the trouble? Given up?"

"What is there to give up?"

"Confidence."

She said in a soft voice, "We're slaves; slaves have no need for confidence."

"I'm not a slave until I feel like a slave."

Something seemed to give way inside of her. Her voice became harsh. "You have no concept of Magarak's reality; you refuse to think; you live by ready-made emotional doctrines — a substitute for thought. What is worse, you try to wrench reality to fit your ideas."

"I've heard all that before," said Barch evenly. "Sometimes the emotional doctrines work out. Do you know why?"

"Why?"

"Because neither you nor I are really pals with reality. We don't know whose emotional doctrine it fits … Anyway — whether it's impossible or not — if there's a way out of this Magarak slave-camp, I'll try to find it — and I'll take you with me if I can." He took hold of her shoulders, squeezed as if to shake her into confidence. With dull annoyance, he noted the quivering of her flesh. He took his hands away.

She said wearily, "Your ideas are — not well-formed. You can't escape Magarak merely because you have the will to escape."

Barch laughed grimly. "I certainly can't escape without it…Those twelve Lenape got loose."

"There's a great difference; they are a highly developed race; they have a feeling for the organization of Magarak. Also, they were in a position to control the growth of the ship on which they escaped."

"Growth?"

"Yes, certainly. Ships are grown, like you Earthers grow cabbages. The Lenape are experts in the techniques of growth-matter; on Lenau they grow their dwellings, their ocean-ships, their air-ships. On Lekthwa much the same is true."

Barch grinned. "That's a point of difference between us. We grow our food and build our space-ships. You grow your ships and build your food."

Komeitk Lelianr said listlessly, "It's easier to grow ships than to build them. When you become proficient in space-ship design you will recognize the advantages."

"Well, cabbages, space-ships, Lenape aside, there are other ways of escape."

"How?" She laughed shortly. "You know nothing of Magarak. You cannot imagine it. It's not a matter of killing a guard, jumping a fence and running."

"I didn't say I'd succeed. I said I'd try."

She smiled. "Yes. The 'dynamic thrust' of your race."

Barch looked at her with near-dislike. "Call it anything you want. Maybe when a race gets old like yours, it gets stale, sour."

"Perhaps." She stretched out her legs, her arms. After a moment she turned her head, looked at him with what seemed new curiosity. "Your optimism is stimulating, in any event."

Barch grinned. Ages ago, Claude Darran had spoken of Barch's capacity for optimism in different terms.

As if following his thoughts, Komeitk Lelianr murmured, "What strange life-lines we weave through the cosmic gel…Three days ago…"

For the first time, Barch saw tears in her eyes.

Time passed.

✳

Without warning, the cell burst open. White light dazzled their eyes; there was a wave of sound, a tumble of black shapes. The white light cut off, the walls were whole. The cell suddenly seemed full of ill-smelling flesh.

Barch pressed back against the wall. There were eight new-comers, six men, two women: squat white creatures with moist bulldog faces. They wore threadbare gray smocks, leather stockings, shoes like blobs of yellow gum.

Komeitk Lelianr said tonelessly, "Kopsari, or perhaps Modoks. I thought it strange the hold was given to us alone."

Warily Barch watched the eight. Their faces showed no emotion, no expression. There was hoarse conversation, then dead silence while all of them inspected Barch and Komeitk Lelianr.

Komeitk Lelianr said with a tinge of interest in her voice, "I would fit them approximately at 14-90, by the Epignotic Cultural Calculation…Notice, the cloth of their garments; durable, shaped rather than woven; their shoes, molded permanently to their feet. These must be outdoor serfs, in the service of what the science calls a *Technics-Lord.*"

Barch made a non-committal sound.

"Not an uncommon pattern around the universe," she went on in a monotone. "Their lot will change little for better or worse."

Barch muttered, "I wonder how much longer we'll be in this hold."

"Are you anxious for Magarak?"

"No, I don't like the smell."

"You might sometime wish yourself back in this cell."

"Do you think they'll separate us?"

"Certainly."

Barch felt a sharp twinge of panic.

She said in a flat voice, "First the slaves are graded at rough intellectual levels; they must pass through a hall filled with traps, pitfalls, obstacles, unpleasant sensations, and the like, which they avoid according to their intelligence. After this first division, the lower grades are classified by physique, agility, dexterity." She looked across the cell. "However, these serfs will probably go out to the mud-flats along Xolboar Sea, a great reclamation project, which uses up thousands of labor-units a year."

"And how about us?"

"A thousand possibilities."

Barch awoke to a sound of harsh voices. He crouched instinctively, slowly relaxed. Two of the blank-faced serfs were fighting, clawing clumsily at each other's faces. The remaining men and the women watched critically.

"Disgusting animals," said Komeitk Lelianr.

One of the contestants suddenly ceased to fight. The other put his legs against the square back, jerked back at the head. The eyes stared up, the neck snapped. There came a sudden raucous babble.

"What are they fighting about?" Barch asked in bewilderment.

"Impossible to say."

"Look…"

The two women were slapping at the man who had conquered, stolidly, without anger. At last he threw up his hands as if in defeat, crossed to a man who had been watching, caught him by the neck, smashed his head against the wall until the skull became like jelly. The women spoke on angrily for a few moments, then appeared to lose interest. No one heeded the limp bodies. There were a few dark glances cast toward Barch and Komeitk Lelianr, one or two monosyllables, then silence.

Barch said speculatively, "I wonder what would happen…" He looked thoughtfully at Komeitk Lelianr. "Offhand, would you say that these creatures will be well-treated on Magarak?"

She examined him curiously. "I have no idea. We know very little of Magarak. I assume that they are not as strictly supervised as the technical workers."

"Suppose the Klau found a body in your clothes and a body in mine…"

Komeitk Lelianr shuddered. "You want me — to wear those clothes?"

"We have nothing to lose, perhaps something to gain."

"But," she shook her head. "I see no reason —"

"If we get sent out to those mud-flats, we go out together!"

"Oh," said Komeitk Lelianr in sudden enlightenment. "The dynamic attitude, this tinkering with destiny…"

"Yes," said Barch grimly. "If I couldn't be doing something, I might as well throw up the sponge... Are you game?"

She shrugged. "It makes no difference."

Barch flushed. "If you'd rather go it alone — say so."

"No, Roy. I don't object to you personally."

"Thanks," growled Barch.

She smiled. "Maybe our friends won't like us undressing their dead."

"Let 'em try to stop me... There'll be eight corpses instead of two."

CHAPTER VIII

HE PUSHED HIMSELF OUT to the nearest body, and with a challenging survey of the six white faces, began to jerk the gray garment loose.

There was an undertone of muttering. Black eyes became beady and thoughtful. No one stirred. Underneath the jacket was a skin-tight coverall of matted fiber. "This is the smallest," said Barch. "Let's have your clothes."

Komeitk Lelianr slipped out of the white and black harlequin costume, climbed gingerly into the gray smock.

Barch stripped the second corpse down to the gray matted undersuit, pulled off his coat and trousers. Closing his nostrils to the sour odor of the garment, he pulled it over his head.

There was motion along the wall. Barch looked up sharply. One of the men was feeling the material of his coat. My good gray flannel, thought Barch. He jerked it away, started to pull it on the corpse.

Now there were mutters. The older of the women made a furious babbling sound; the other made a gesture with stiff fingers against her lips. Barch ignored the noise, buttoned the coat, began to pull the legs into the trousers. The legs were too short, the cuffs dragged ridiculously over the yellow blobs of wax or resin that covered the dead man's feet.

From the corner of his eye he saw Komeitk Lelianr deftly thrusting the second body into her black and white costume. She buckled her pouch under the gray smock, then bringing forth her atomizer, sprayed the dead face, the coarse hair to a dull beige tone.

Barch critically inspected her gleaming silver hair. "You don't make a very good peasant."

He looked around the cell. One of the Modoks wore a loose conical cap. Barch pushed himself forward, reached out, took the cap. The man half-heartedly clutched for the cap, then backed away, eyes staring with frantic alarm.

The women babbled in approval.

Barch yanked the cap down on Komeitk Lelianr's hair. "There," he inspected her, "that's a little better." He turned to look at their cellmates. "They're certainly an odd-acting bunch…"

"It's all relative," said Komeitk Lelianr. "They undoubtedly think the same of us."

Barch looked down at his shoes, at Komeitk Lelianr's sandals. "Do you think we'll pass?"

"I couldn't say."

The ship shivered; they heard deep clanking sounds, like an anchor-chain running down a hawse-pipe. "What's that?"

"I don't know… Perhaps we have arrived."

"If so — we didn't get changed any too soon."

The ship jarred; the red glow in the wall pulsed bright and dim. A moment later the cell burst open. Gravity seized at the ten bodies — eight living, two dead. They slid down the cell wall, together with all the accumulated litter, trash and refuse, down a smooth chute. Fresh air was cold on their faces; sound roared at their ears.

Barch's eyes smarted under the sudden light, his legs felt limp at the knees. "Ellen!" he cried. "Ellen, where are you?"

Blinking, he looked around him. They stood in a fenced enclosure, like a cattle pen. Komeitk Lelianr was a few feet distant, holding to her cap, which the original owner was attempting to reclaim. Barch staggered over, smote the man with his fist.

Something stung at his back, burning like fire; he turned snarling. Above him, on a ramp, stood a tremendous man with blood-red skin. Black spikes of hair extended like quills six inches to all sides of his head. He had eyes with red four-starred centers like the Klau and he carried a tube with a flickering serpent of light darting up, down, in, out.

He roared at Barch in a voice like a brass horn, flourished the flail. A disturbance in the adjoining pen attracted his attention. He pounded down the ramp. The flickering light-snake curled out. Barch heard a sharp cry.

He gained Komeitk Lelianr's side, dazed and angry, shook his head as if to clear it of confusion, glowered up at the trumpeting red whip-wielders.

Directly overhead a hatch opened; a stream of bodies plummeted at him. He jumped aside, pushed Komeitk Lelianr against the fence, away from the milling center of the pen, and here he caught his breath.

The ship continued to discharge. Men and women tumbled, slid, spewed from orifices under the ship, their fall broken by the bawling bodies below.

Past the great hulk Barch glimpsed the shapes of two other ships. Beyond rose the facade of a building a mile high, the roof-line blurred in fog. There was a steady roar in the air, like the sound of surf; a smell of mud, rust, ammonia hung across the pens.

Komeitk Lelianr said coolly in his ear, "We're part of a not-too-valuable cargo. We'll be worked very hard, we'll die very quickly."

He looked at her truculently. "You sound as if you don't care."

"I know what to expect. This is Magarak."

Barch said, "Personally, I'm scared stiff."

She shrugged. "Adjust yourself, your fear will pass."

Barch glared. "Adjust myself be damned! I'm mostly afraid that I won't be able to make these devils regret the day they saw me."

She glanced up to the top of the ramp. "The Podruods will soon cure you of that."

"They have eyes like the Klau."

"They're a sub-species of Klau. There are Big Klau, Little Klau, Bornghalese, Podruods — all Klau stock. The Podruods are the troops, the guards, the fighters."

A metallic clatter rang out accompanied by distant shouts. Barch, turning his head, saw a long feather-shaped boom vibrating back and forth across the sky. Overhead six white balls snapped past — one after the other, like rockets.

He said in Komeitk Lelianr's ears, "This is bedlam."

She nodded briefly. "Compared to other parts of Magarak it's quiet."

The Podruod voice rang out above like a clarion. "Hey! Hey! Hey!" Directly behind the fence opened.

"I guess we move," muttered Barch.

A sudden rush of gray bodies with frightened white faces surged past. Knobby shoulders pummelled Barch. "Ellen!" he cried. "Ellen!" He looked all around desperately. "Ellen! Where are you? Ellen! Ellen!"

Arms thrust angrily at him, he was carried along the tide. "Ellen!" He thought he heard his name; he stopped to listen. Nothing but the shuffle and thud of feet, ringing shouts of the great red Podruods.

A chute loomed ahead. Four abreast the Modoks scuttled up, jumped down into what appeared to be a long black barge. A Podruod with legs painted blue stood in the stern, his face working like rubber, yelling, crying.

Barch craned his neck, searching the sea of alien faces. Fifty feet ahead he saw Komeitk Lelianr. "Ellen!" She turned her head. A great red hand obscured her face; she stumbled up the chute.

A second chute opened at Barch's right; the Podruods roared new directions.

Barch pushed forward, now shoving against the tide. He saw Komeitk Lelianr half-way up the chute. The Podruod roared, struck at him; the light-serpent snapped out.

Barch fell to his knees; feet pressed around him, stepping on his hands, his legs.

He crawled doggedly through, saw massive Podruod legs ahead. In sudden fury, he dove forward, tackled the legs. The great body toppled; the light-whip rolled in the dust. Barch snatched at it, missed. He rose to his feet, raced up the chute, pressed into the last of the group.

From behind came a hoarse yelling; Barch glancing over his shoulder, saw a clot of Modoks kicking at the great spiked head, smiling, laughing.

Podruods came pounding along the ramp; light-snakes darted; the gray men dutifully marched into the chutes. The red man writhed, kicked on the ground like a beetle on its back.

Barch pushed ahead. "Ellen!" He grasped her arm. "I thought I had lost you."

She took his hand, squeezed it tight. Barch's heart gave a sudden throb of joy. It was almost worth coming to Magarak.

A gate clanged behind them. The barge shuddered, rose into the air, slid clear of the slave-yard.

Barch and Komeitk Lelianr, the last aboard, leaned against the rail.

Komeitk Lelianr motioned across the panorama. "Now — look at Magarak…"

Chapter IX

THE SCENE WAS TOO VAST, too complex for mental grasp. Barch sensed flaring lights, gigantic objects in motion, monstrous shapes. Near at hand the lights were like openings into furnaces: yellow, orange, green-white, red; at the horizon they gleamed and flickered like stars.

Heavy sound came at a constant grumbling pitch, so far-reaching that it seemed an intrinsic property of the planet. Across the sky moved endless shapes — booms swinging in slow circles, black objects like spiders darting along glistening tracks, barges floating at various levels, blasts of dark vapor. Then underneath were the buildings: gray-white, greenish-gray, black, orange-black, some faintly etched with window lines, others blank as new paper. Between were dark crevasses flickering with yellow or bluish glow far at the bottom.

Barch looked up into the sky, smoky, sooty, lumpy with low clouds. "Is it day or night?... It must be day."

Komeitk Lelianr asked wryly, "What do you think of Magarak?"

"I feel like an ant in a thrashing-machine," said Barch. He looked around the horizon. "How far does the madhouse go on?"

"We must be on Kdoa," she mused. "A large continent — about five thousand of your miles wide."

"Five thousand miles of — this!"

She nodded. "Underneath are the barracks, the commissaries, the nurseries."

"Nurseries — for what?"

"Slave-children. Slaves are encouraged to breed. The women become pregnant often to avoid heavy work. The children make the best slaves; they know no other kind of life."

Barch silently watched the shapes and lights of Magarak drift past below.

"Do you still think you can —" she nodded "— defeat this?"

Barch looked at her resentfully. "Do you think I won't try?"

"No. I think you'll try. I think you'll end up on the grid." She added tonelessly, "That's where the slaves are punished."

Below them wound a dull brown river; in the distance Barch saw the leaden gleam of open water. "Is that Xolboar?"

"I'm not sure. In our schooling we learn the geography of many worlds, but I can't remember Magarak too well."

Barch stared over the side. Another barge drifted toward them, passed two hundred feet below. Barch saw six long dark shapes, like spindles, caught the white flash of upturned faces. The barges drifted apart.

The sea spread leaden, listless; they drifted over dreary mud-flats. Ahead appeared a long black line which, as the barge drew near, broke up into clots of men, piles of cut stone, spidery cranes. A coffer dam of mud had been scraped up against the sea; in deep oozing pits, workers, moving slow as cold ants, fitted great stones together.

"That's what you'll be doing," said Komeitk Lelianr in a flat voice.

Barch stared down into the dismal pits. "And what happens to the women?"

"Some other kind of work. Chipping stones, perhaps."

"If they separate us — we'll never see each other again."

"Does it matter? This is Magarak."

"It matters to me."

"Hard workers are allowed to visit the female barracks. Breeding is a reward for hard work. Perhaps you will chance upon me in the stalls." She looked around the raft, at the dough-faced creatures in the gray jerkins. "I would rather have you than one of them."

"Thanks," said Barch bitterly. "You overwhelm me."

They passed a barge loaded with stone. Barch asked, "What keeps these barges up? Do they use the same machinery as the space-ships?"

"I would imagine so." Her voice was disinterested. "The principle of plane-cohesion is fundamental."

"But they could leave the planet?"

"I suppose so." She watched the reclamation project fall astern. "We're not bound there, at least..."

The ocean shore curved away behind them; a range of mountains loomed dark ahead. The sky was darkening rapidly. The sun had settled beyond the overcast. "I wonder how much farther?" asked Barch.

Komeitk Lelianr knit her brows. "If those mountains are the Palamkum, then that was Tchul Sea, and this is Kredbon instead of Kdoa. I think Xolboar Sea is beyond those mountains."

"Then we get sorted out, and put to work?"

"I suppose so."

Barch examined the mountains with interest. They were great masses of white rock, split by deep valleys and gorges. Black vegetation carpeted the valley slopes; snow gleamed on the high cols and slopes.

Barch said in a hushed voice, "Can your shoes hold up both of us?"

She looked at him first in startled wonder, then speculatively. "No."

"Suppose we jumped off the raft."

"If I could stay on my feet — we'd drop slowly."

"We'd never be caught down there."

She stared down into the dark wilderness. "We'd starve to death."

"Maybe, maybe not... At least we would be free. We'd be out of the mudpits, out of the breeding-barracks."

She glanced at the Modoks, made up her mind. "Very well. Try to put your feet on top of mine."

Barch looked over the side. They flew over a long valley. "Now," muttered Barch. "Are you ready?"

"Yes."

"Now!" He jumped up, straddled the rail. Komeitk Lelianr climbed nimbly after. Startled white faces turned. There was an excited chatter, a couple of arms tentatively outstretched.

Barch bared his teeth, kicked. The commotion attracted the eye of the Podruod controller. With great lunging strides he came forward.

"I'm ready," panted Komeitk Lelianr. "Step on my feet."

Barch jumped down, clasped her around the waist; they toppled off into gray air. He glimpsed the rectangular hull of the raft slipping past overhead with a hundred little nubbins of heads silhouetted against the twilight. Sky and mountains whirled in sickening topsy-turvy motion.

Komeitk Lelianr was crying in his ear. "My feet, my feet!"

Barch clamped his legs around hers, set his feet on her instep. He felt a braking, the sky and mountains steadied.

Looking anxiously aloft he saw the raft drifting quietly on; the cargo was fuzzy gray, like a load of jute. He turned his eyes down. A massive crag, like a rotten tooth, stabbed up at them with frightening velocity; below was the vast slot of valley, the shining trickle of a river.

"We're dropping fast." He looked into her face. It was clenched in frowning concentration, as she balanced on the shifting angles of force under her feet.

"We're braking," she said. "The lower we get, the slower we fall."

Barch relaxed, tried to follow her as she shifted weight. He became acutely conscious of the feel of her body in his hands — warm, flexible, quick... Dark fronds of vegetation reached up at them. Thirty feet — twenty feet — ten feet...

There was the crash, scatter, agitation of breaking stems and snapping branches. Barch saw the ground, the black humus of the hillside; at six feet he jumped, so as not to land with Komeitk Lelianr's feet under his. She cried out in surprise. Relieved of Barch's weight, she bounced back into the air. She caught at branches, swung back and forth like an acrobat, then slowly settled.

Barch caught her as she came down, kissed her. She submitted quietly, sighing.

Barch's head went light; a ferment of exultation rose up in him. Now he would fight this world single-handed; he would move heaven and earth; his feats would be fables for the future; Komeitk Lelianr would be proud; they would — abruptly she pushed him away, stood looking off into the forest. Barch anxiously moved forward, then held himself, waited.

CHAPTER X

PRESENTLY SHE TURNED BACK. In the dimness of mingled shadow and twilight, Barch could not read her face.

In a controlled voice she said, "It is clear to me that former distinctions are now artificial."

They were in the first place, thought Barch so intensely that he felt she must hear.

"We're on a common level," she went on in a low voice. "We're alone, we've nothing to look forward to —"

"That's wrong," Barch protested. "There's everything ahead of us! I'd rather be here with you than back in San Francisco without you."

She seemed to be smiling. "Anyway, here we are. Regardless of my personal prejudices, I'll have to adjust to the inevitable."

Barch stood back scowling. "What kind of characterization is that?"

She shrugged. "I hardly know. Without thinking I drop into whatever suits the moment."

Barch thought, she can't be blamed for her upbringing; something of what she said was true: the chances of long life were not too good. The feel of her against his chest was still warm, urgent. He reached for her again; she submitted conscientiously. Disturbing ideas darted around Barch's mind like bats; he closed his mind to them, and presently they vanished.

The sky was a black ceiling; dank wind blew roaring through the valley. Trees flapped and clattered; from the far distance came a harsh gurgling whistle. Komeitk Lelianr whispered, "What's that?"

Barch said, "It's breakfast, if I can catch it."

"In the dark it might catch you."

They looked down the slope, found the river. "We'll be warmer up here," said Barch, "out of the valley. We'd better not build a fire until we learn more about the country."

In a little hollow under a rock he piled moss, dry humus, and contrived a covering of fronds wrenched down from the trees. "Like sleeping in a haystack," said Barch. "You get in first."

Rain fell during the night, but the wind blew it over the rock, and they stayed dry. Magarak morning came damp and gray.

"Ouch!" said Barch, "my aching bones." He felt his face. "Thank the lord, no whiskers. I've got your father to thank for that."

Komeitk Lelianr sat brushing the moss off her gray smock.

Barch went on cheerfully. "Next — breakfast. Are you hungry?"

She made no answer.

Barch rose to his feet, looked carefully up and down the hillside. The trees by daylight were like kelp: black and brown, with red veins along the leaves. Overhead the sky swam heavy with clouds.

Barch pulled down a branch, broke free a cluster of nuts. He broke one of these open, smelled, recoiled from the acrid odor. "No nourishment here…Let's see what's down by the river."

Halfway down he stopped short. "I smell smoke."

Komeitk Lelianr raised her head. "I don't smell anything."

"Does anyone live in these hills?"

"I don't know."

"If there were," said Barch, "maybe we could learn what and where to eat."

Komeitk Lelianr suddenly looked as if she were about to cry. Barch said, "Now, now, what's the trouble?"

"Living seems so futile."

"Futile? We're just getting started!"

"But how will we end up? We'll starve, we'll freeze. If anyone sees us, they'll hunt us like animals."

"We'll put up quite a fight first," said Barch. "In the meantime —" kissing her forehead, he pretended not to notice that she pulled back a trifle "— we'll never be any worse off."

Komeitk Lelianr laughed weakly. "No."

"Now, let's see what kind of country we're in."

Cautiously they approached the river. Standing in a pool was a blackish-green creature with the head of an owl, a bat's wings, the legs of a heron. It watched them approach, then fluttered up, flapped croaking off down the valley.

"That's a good sign," said Barch. "It means that there's something to be caught. That bird wasn't just taking a bath."

"We catch things — then eat them?"

"We're savages now," said Barch airily. "Both of us, remember?"

"I remember very well."

Barch crept toward the pool, over glistening dark rocks. Komeitk Lelianr remained aloof, her face turned away.

Barch stared into the pool. Water swirled quietly over round stones of various colors. Things like trifoil spirals wriggled through the water. Too small, thought Barch. He scanned the bottom. One of the round stones moved. Barch grabbed shoulder-deep into water like ice, came up with a squirming bulb. Dangling tentacles flapped, wound around his wrist; his skin burned as if singed with flame. Barch cursed, threw the bulb up on the shore. It scuttled toward the river. Barch kicked it back, dropped a chunk of rock on it. When he picked up the rock, there was nothing below but a mat of whitish fibers and ooze.

Barch turned away in disgust. A red weal had formed along his wrist, the bones of his forearm ached. "Let's go on downstream," he said through his teeth. "Maybe we'll find something a little less hard to get along with."

The river flowed smoothly a hundred yards, then began to drop. It pounded over step-like ledges, split itself against boulders. Scrambling over the wet rocks, Barch almost fell a dozen times. Glancing over his shoulder, he saw Komeitk Lelianr walking serenely two or three feet over the river.

Said Barch quizzically, "I wish I had a pair of those sandals."

Komeitk Lelianr made no reply.

"How long will the power hold out?" asked Barch.

"With steady use, perhaps a month or two."

"And how high can you walk?"

"Two or three hundred feet. Higher, if I take care."

"Suppose you walk up fifty feet, and tell me what you see."

Swaying and stepping as if walking on stilts, she rose into the air. The wind caught her, carried her drifting down the valley.

Barch scrambled over the rocks to keep abreast. "What do you see?"

"Rocks, more black trees, a lake."

"No smoke? No buildings?"

"Nothing." She came back down in great sliding steps. "Do you think we'll find anything to eat?"

"Of course," Barch said confidently. "Down by the lake, perhaps."

A few minutes later the valley widened. Before them spread the lake, roughly circular, surrounded first by a rim of marsh, then a strip of open slope over-grown with thorny bush. Each bush terminated in a tight green sac, like a green-gage. Barch picked one, split it, smelled of the pulp. "Rather like lemon verbena, or bay rum."

Komeitk Lelianr said in practical tones, "It's likely to be poisonous."

Barch smelled again, doubtfully. "One can't hurt me too much…"

"It might make you sick."

"Then we'll know it's poison; there's nothing like the empirical method." He bit into the sac, chewed thoughtfully. "It doesn't taste very good."

"Look," said Komeitk Lelianr, "there's that flying thing again."

Barch dropped the thorn berry, watched the owl-headed, bat-winged, heron-legged creature slide to an awkward landing along the shore of the lake.

"If we can catch him," said Barch, "we'll have roast owl." He bent, picked up a rock, moved cautiously forward.

The owl-bat-heron waded out into the lake — stopped short, one leg high in the air. The leg stabbed forward, jerked forward, jerked back up; a black shape twisted through the air, fell into the thorny thicket.

"That looks like a fish," exclaimed Barch. The owl-bat stalked toward his catch. Barch ran forward, waving his arms. "No you don't." Gingerly he picked the black fish out of the thorns, while the owl-bat scuttled back into the water. Komeitk Lelianr watched with distaste.

Barch tossed her his cigarette lighter. "You build a fire, I'll clean this thing."

He set it on a flat rock beside the river, sawed off head and tail with a sharp flake of stone. Gritting his teeth, he split open the soft belly, pulled, scraped, washed, and eventually had two strips of leathery white flesh.

Komeitk had started a fire by the edge of the forest; Barch secured a pair of green twigs, carefully roasted the fish for them.

"There," he said, "that smells pretty good." He laid the fish on a rock, licked his fingers. "It even tastes good."

Komeitk Lelianr ate without comment.

"It's not too filling," said Barch, "but we won't starve today." He looked back to the green thorn-berries. "They didn't taste good — but I don't feel any pangs yet." He covered over the fire. "Now we'd better explore."

A distant explosion jarred the air. Echoes rumbled away down the valley. "What's that?"

"It's called blasting," Komeitk Lelianr explained indifferently. "An unstable substance is confined, then —"

Barch said sourly, "We poor savages are not entirely ignorant of explosives. In fact we make a pretty good one out of uranium."

Komeitk Lelianr stood listening. "Probably there's a stone quarry somewhere over a mountain."

Barch anxiously scanned the mountain-side. "We've got to explore, find out where the nearest settlement is, if there is one."

"And then what?"

"We'll know more when we see how the land lies. If we could steal one of those barges somehow we might…" His voice trailed off into silence. He caught Komeitk Lelianr, pulled her down behind a thorn-bush. "Quiet!"

Across the lake three men stood like pillars of gray rock.

"They've seen us," whispered Komeitk Lelianr.

"I don't think so. I saw them come out of the forest."

"If they come around this way, they'll see us."

"They're coming." Barch took round heavy stones in each hand, waited tensely for them.

CHAPTER XI

TWO OF THE MEN were dark-skinned, with faces thin and fox-like; the third was lemon-yellow, with a flat round face, orange eyebrows tufted like horns. They moved with a soft stealthy tread that suggested the wariness of deer.

"They've got bows and arrows," muttered Barch. "They can't be either slaves or keepers."

"Perhaps they're fugitives too," said Komeitk Lelianr.

The men drew closer, the sound of their voices came across the marsh. Through the thorns Barch could see every detail of their faces, their clothes. Twenty yards away they stopped short, turned to look down the valley.

Faint in the distance came a sound like a bugle-call, then another from a different direction, then another, startlingly close. The three men hissed in sudden fright, bounded off up the hillside, disappeared under the blanket of black fronds.

Barch uneasily rose to his feet, looked across the lake. "Whatever it is, it's certainly not good…We'd better leave too."

Komeitk Lelianr seized his ankle. "Get down," she whispered, "Podruods!"

Barch dropped flat on his face. Out of the forest sprang a lithe red figure. He stood poised, raised his spiked head, called; bugle tones rang across the lake.

He waited. Answering calls like hunting-horns returned from the distance.

The Podruod stood like a statue; Barch and Komeitk Lelianr hugged the marshy ground.

There was a crashing of branches, thudding of hasty feet. A fat man with a conical tuft of pink hair stumbled into the clearing. He saw the Podruod, froze like a bird. The Podruod watched him without moving a muscle. The fat man cautiously started to slip around the lake. The Podruod made a leap forward, halted. Barch thought of a cat with a mouse.

The Podruod once more raised his head, again the brass voice rang out. Behind the fat man two more Podruods jumped into the clearing. The fat man ran frantically, panting and groaning.

A shadow passed over Barch's head; he looked up with a convulsive jerk that hurt his neck. It was a raft ten feet long, four feet wide, carrying a Klau. If the Klau had looked down he might have seen Barch and Komeitk Lelianr, but his eyes were on the fat man.

Under the raft hung a dark mass, like a bundle of clothes; as the raft slid forward it unfolded, lowered arms like lengths of black hose. They coiled around the fugitive's chest, his legs, his ankles. He stumbled, fell into the thorn-bushes where he lay kicking, thrashing, screaming like a horse.

The raft moved slowly on, dragged him through the bushes, across the mud, into the lake. He sank out of sight. The surface of the lake rippled and boiled. The raft rose; the fat man now hung limp. He was covered with round brown cups. One by one they dropped away, splashed back into the lake. Barch recognized the stinger-molluscs which had jarred his arm. He squeezed himself even flatter into the ground.

The black arms contracted, the fat man was hoisted up, a black mantle dropped in limp folds around him, pinched in at the bottom, became a tight bag.

The raft rose, slid quietly down the valley. Barch turned to look for the Podruods. They had vanished.

He lay flaccid for a moment, then glanced at Komeitk Lelianr. Her eyes were glassy. He nudged her, said in a husky whisper, "Let's run for the trees."

She lay like warm wax, breathing shallowly. Barch gained his feet, scraped the mud from his heels, stood with his knees loose and shaking. He lifted Komeitk Lelianr; half-carried her into the darkness of the forest.

✳

They sat for ten minutes, Komeitk Lelianr resting limply on Barch's chest. He stroked her hair, kissed her forehead. Presently she sighed, sat up. Barch asked anxiously, "Feeling better?"

"Yes."

Barch rose to his feet, looked up the hillside where the first three men had taken refuge. "Let's try up there; we might learn something."

Komeitk Lelianr rose passively to her feet. Barch asked, "Are you rested?"

"Yes."

They slowly climbed the hill. Long red-veined black fronds fell around them like weeping willows. They could not see, they could not be seen. On the heavy humus their feet made no sound. Every moment or so Barch stopped to listen. Silence.

Light punctured the wall of fronds. The hillside levelled off, dipped into a basin. The humus thinned, revealing chalky white marl underneath.

Barch heard a quick breath; he spun on his heel. Behind stood a grinning Podruod with a shaved head, wearing a black breech clout and black boots. Slowly, with a fanciful flourish he extended his arm; a sliver of bright steel nearly touched Barch's chest. Barch's eyes shifted behind to a second man, slender, yellowish-white of skin, who had seized Komeitk Lelianr's arms from behind.

Barch hesitated. The Podruod's metallic voice rang out peremptorily. Barch made no reply. He spoke again, this time with harsh emphasis. Barch saw the muscles tense to stab; dimly heard Komeitk Lelianr answering in the same tongue. The Podruod relaxed; death moved back a pace.

The Podruod turned to Komeitk Lelianr, looked her over, up and down. He spoke again; Komeitk Lelianr replied.

"What's he saying?" Barch demanded.

Komeitk Lelianr said in a distant voice, "They want to know if there are any more of us. They're escaped slaves too. The Podruod must be a criminal of some sort."

"Oh." Barch relaxed. "Is that all?"

Komeitk Lelianr said non-committally, "Most of it."

"What do you mean?"

"There seems a kind of tribe living up here." She nodded at the Podruod. "He's the chief."

The Podruod's inspection of Komeitk Lelianr suddenly aroused Barch's apprehension. He said in a hurried monotone, "Throw on the power in your shoes. He's not holding you tightly; you can break away. I'll take off down hill."

Komeitk Lelianr frowned, turned a side-glance at the red man. "We'd be better off here than starving to death alone."

"No," said Barch desperately. "I'll take care of you."

The Podruod with a quick motion sheathed his rapier. He motioned on ahead, pushed Barch's shoulder with a heavy hand.

Shame, rage overcame Barch; he swung a punch. The Podruod grinned, ducked back. The sliver of steel gleamed in the air; he lunged playfully; a quarter inch of steel stabbed Barch's shoulder. Pale with anger and frustration Barch jerked back.

"Roy," cried Komeitk Lelianr, "be sensible! Obey him, or you'll be killed!"

"He's got his eyes on you," panted Barch. "Once we get in that cave, I can't protect you; he'll take you…"

Komeitk Lelianr said wearily, "What's the difference? I've already reconciled myself…"

The steel menaced again; the Podruod barked out roughly. With an agonizing sickness in the pit of his stomach, Barch stumbled forward. "What's the difference?" she had said. The chief was a red-skinned savage, Barch was a light-tan savage. "What's the difference?"

They crossed an open flat, climbed a little slope to the wall of a sheer limestone cliff. The yellow-white man motioned Komeitk Lelianr into a shadowed indentation. At the far end Barch saw a narrow crevice. The first man and Komeitk Lelianr slid into the crevice. Barch followed, groped along a short irregular passage, stumbled into a low-ceilinged hall close after the girl.

Smoky yellow lamps and a blazing fire gave off warm light; there were two rough tables, benches, the smell of food and bodies. Twenty or thirty men and women were visible; others came blinking curiously out of dark corners.

Barch stood tensely, his eyes on Komeitk Lelianr. He muttered feverishly to himself, she never cared for me any more than I care for a dog…I'm just Roy, a good dog. She reconciled herself to me, now what's the difference? There she stood, slender, so lovely and golden that he could see nothing else…She was looking not at Barch, but at the Podruod.

Barch followed her gaze. The chief was giving directions to a pair of men in gray; he turned, called across the cave to where a pot bubbled on the fire. He stood three inches more than six feet: a magnificent creature, wide, thick, without a spare ounce of flesh. His head was shaved; he had hard bony features, and walked in his heavy black boots as lightly as Lekthwans walked on air-sandals. Barch looked anxiously back to Komeitk Lelianr. She still watched the chief; the lamplight reflected flickering in her eyes.

The chief walked over to her, put his hands on her shoulders. She shrank back, but not, thought Barch, as far as she had shrunk from him.

Barch, oblivious to everything except two shapes, walked quietly forward. The chief's back was turned. Komeitk Lelianr saw him coming without expression.

The chief turned, negligently reached for his rapier. Barch caught it, yanked it free; it fell tinkling against the stone.

The chief kicked at Barch; Barch seized the foot, pulled. The chief staggered back, hopping with great agility on one foot.

Barch charged forward, stopped a great open-handed slap. He punched, felt the numb jar of blows. Lamps, walls, fires, faces became a meaningless backdrop. The red face was intent, the nostrils flared. Barch twisted the face askew with a haymaker; the face twisted back without change of expression. Barch felt his wind going, his legs felt like logs, he could hardly raise his arms.

"Ellen," he croaked, "grab a rock, brain him…"

Komeitk Lelianr pressed back against the wall, turned her face away. Three great blows hit Barch. The first was like a lead hammer and the lights faded. The second was like a dark surf washing over him, the third was a rumble of distant thunder.

Chapter XII

Barch awoke on a pile of skins. He sat up, feeling his face. It was puffy and ached dully. At a long table across the room three or four women pounded meal in stone mortars.

At the end sat Komeitk Lelianr. She rose to her feet, bent over a pot, came to Barch with a crockery bowl. "Eat this and you'll feel better."

Barch started to speak, but the words choked in his throat. He took the bowl, drank. Komeitk Lelianr stood watching. Barch said politely, "Nothing more, thank you."

She turned away, then looked back over her shoulder. "Roy, you must learn to think realistically, to limit your idealism by possibility."

"I will," said Barch, "when I'm sure of what's impossible." He handed back the bowl, stared at her coldly. "How're you making out with your new man?"

"Clet?" She shrugged.

"You speak his same language I notice."

"It's a kind of common tongue that everyone knows."

Barch turned his head to the wall. A few minutes later he rose to his feet, staggered outside, leaned against the cliff, vomited.

Raising his head again, he saw a pair of gray men skirting the hillside, carrying a basket between them. Behind came Clet, the Podruod chief, a beast the size of a boar slung over his shoulder. His eyes fixed impassively on Barch, he strode inside the cave.

Barch settled himself upon a rock, rubbed his aching head. After a moment he raised his eyes, studied the expanse of the valley. It was shaped roughly like the Mediterranean Sea, with the cave at a position comparable to Libya. High mountains ringed the Levantine end; at

Gibraltar the river cut through a narrow steep-walled notch; along the Côte d'Azur he noticed the entrance to a second valley. Directly opposite the cave, in the position of Italy, a great round-knobbed bluff reared up to dominate the valley. Strange, thought Barch, that the Klau maintain no fort up there. Looking closely he thought to see the outline of ruins.

Overcast scudded low over the mountains; a few drops of rain fell. Barch rose to his feet, shivered as a cold blast of wind penetrated the threadbare Modok garment.

He looked tentatively toward the crevice into the cave — inside were Clet and Komeitk Lelianr. He growled wordlessly, walked down the slope away from the cave.

He stopped short. Angrily he asked himself, can't I take it? Am I afraid to go back in? He turned around, marched through the rain back into the cave. The two men with the basket now sat beside it husking a kind of nut. One of them snapped his fingers at Barch, motioned.

Barch glowered, half-turned away. But, he decided, he would look less of a fool working than refusing to work. He could always leave the cave — but why should he? He was free; he was fed and sheltered; there was no reason for him to go, except his outraged vanity. He glanced around the cavern. Neither Clet nor Komeitk Lelianr were in sight.

Barch sat down, began hulling nuts.

Weeks passed, two, three, a month. Barch mastered the simple routines of the tribe, gained a smattering of the common tongue. On several occasions he went hunting, and once killed a large brown two-legged creature like a hybrid of kangaroo and lizard, for which he was warmly congratulated.

He explored the cave. Four different passages opened out of the community hall. Two struck off more or less horizontally, winding through small chambers, chapels, nooks, niches and alcoves wherein the tribesmen slept. A third led down past Clet's chamber, dropping into the depths under the mountain. The fourth served as a flue for the fire, led up into an enormous space over the hall called Big Hole. At one end, where the wall was barely a shell, daylight seeped in through a fissure. Stalactites hung, stalagmites rose, occasionally joining to form spindly columns of fascinating height. In Big Hole, Barch arranged his bed of humus and rudely cured hides.

The tribe numbered thirty-four: twenty-one men, ten women, three doubtfuls. These last were the Calbyssinians: Armian, Ardl, Arn, whose sex was a frantically guarded secret. They were slight pretty creatures with melting blue eyes and purple-gold hair. They bundled themselves in loose cloaks, and spent all their leisure time trying to probe out each other's secret. The hints, wiles, sly strategies provided Barch with almost his only amusement.

In addition to the Calbyssinians, there were five Byathids: four tall pink men with foxy eyes, droopy noses, silky cinnamon-colored hair; one pink raw-boned woman with a voice like a sheep.

There was Kerbol, stocky and gray-green with a pointed head, a face like a frog, with his dour woman.

There were three hatchet-faced Splangs with skins like Cordovan leather: Chevrr, Skurr and a thin beetle-faced woman that they shared.

There were two Griffits, cat-like men with watchful sidelong eyes, stiff mustaches and an air of vindictive truculence that never quite manifested itself.

There was a large brown man who had lost his nose; his name was Flatface. He controlled two bald and bad-tempered women of un-guessable race. There was Pedratz, taffy-colored and smelling of musk, with eyebrows that rose into fantastic horns. There was Moranko, a sullenly handsome youth who hated Clet and presently Barch. There was the dwarf Moses, with a Punchinello face and skin like a piebald horse.

There were six of the bulldog-faced Modoks: four men and two women. They crouched by themselves at the back of the hall, watching everything with wide suspicious eyes.

There was Sl, a white-skinned man with white bifurcated beard and split nose who did everything double; there was the musician Lkandeli Szet. There was Barch; there was Clet and his three women: Komeitk Lelianr and a pair of young nondescripts who had been the original property of Lkandeli Szet.

Making a mental inventory, Barch estimated that at least fifteen races from as many worlds occupied the cave. Sitting quietly at the back bench, he considered the mélange with wry amusement. Never would it be said that his life had been uneventful or drab.

On Earth no one even suspected the existence of Magarak. And yet by this time...With a queasiness in his stomach, he speculated on the Klau raid. What had been their purpose?

Across the hall the voices of Flatface's two bald women rose in acrimony. Clet, at the big table in front of the fire, raised his bony red head; the bickering quieted. Clet disliked noise. Here was one reason, thought Barch, for the fact that the tribe so widely disparate in background could live in comparative amity. Another lay in the fundamental nature of their existence, a kind of cultural least-common-denominator, a stage through which each of the races had passed. For Barch, that stage had been only three or four thousand years in the past. He glanced at Komeitk Lelianr, who sat drawing aimless patterns on the table with her fingers. How long had it been since her ancestors lived in caves? A hundred thousand years? A million?

She looked clean and fresh, Barch noticed. Her face was thinner; her mouth had lost something of its girlish curve. Her expression was abstracted, distant, the result of a stoic or fatalistic characterization, Barch decided.

Slowly she looked up. Her eyes rested an instant on Clet. Her eyebrows flickered, but her face showed no change.

Barch rose to his feet, went outside into the darkness. Mist that was not quite drizzle dampened his face. Against the blurred gray of the limestone cliff he noticed a dark shape. His heart stopped for an instant, then started again. It was Kerbol, whom nature had endowed with a skin the color of wet rock, pop-eyes, a mouth like a flap. Barch remembered that Kerbol grumbled about the heat in the hall and seemed to enjoy the cool dampness of the valley.

Barch went to stand beside him; any man that preferred the solitude of the valley to the hall seemed an ally.

Kerbol grunted, and after a moment said in a deep rumbling voice, "The mist falls, the wind blows backwards down Palkwarkz Ztvo. Tomorrow the sky will be high and then the Klau come hunting. Tomorrow will be a good day to stay close by the cave."

Barch remembered the bugling Podruods, the frantic fat man, the

Klau raft with the black arms dangling below. "How often do the Klau hunt?"

"Every eight, ten days, if the weather suits. They are the Quodaras District Klau; Palkwarkz Ztvo is their region. The Xolboar Klau hunt in Poriflammes." He pointed to the valley entering the Palkwarkz Ztvo near the mouth.

Sudden enlightenment came to Barch. "So — we live in a hunting preserve; we're tolerated in order to provide the Klau sport!"

"The Klau planet is a week distant; the Klau must amuse themselves."

Barch said thoughtfully, "I could certainly amuse myself hunting Podruods and Klau."

Kerbol digested the idea. "You think in strange directions. Very strange."

Barch laughed sourly. "I don't see anything strange about it. If the Klau hunt me, it's only fair that I hunt them."

"That is not the theory of the hunt." Kerbol spoke politely.

"It's not the Klau theory, it is my theory. Do we have to live by Klau theory?"

"It is a Klau planet; the Klau brought us here."

Barch grinned. "You escaped, you came here. Is that good Klau theory?"

Kerbol said thoughtfully, "It was too hot at the quarry."

A dull explosion from over Kebali Ridge jarred the air of the valley. "There they shoot now," said Kerbol. "Notice the double shock?"

"No."

"The charge was ten cans of abiloid, a twentieth cut of the Super. The Super smashes the rock, the abiloid pushes it down."

"You seem to know a great deal about explosives."

Kerbol nodded gloomily. "Five years I drilled and charged, drilled and charged. And always in the heat. I ran into the forest, and came over Mount Kebali to Palkwarkz Ztvo, where I must take my chances with the hunters."

Barch asked curiously, "What is that black thing that hangs under the Klau raft?"

"Those are —" Kerbol stopped, grasped for a word "— pulling-things. In factories they lift loads. The Klau grow them, they are half-alive."

"The Klau carry other weapons?"

"Yes. They shoot across long distances; a little splinter enters a man's belly, explodes. The man is dead."

Barch looked up and down the dark valley. The mist had risen, a current of air smelling of rotting vegetation blew on his face. From the far distance sounded a harsh clanking, a screech. Barch muttered, "At night a whole regiment of Podruods could come up here."

Kerbol moved uneasily. "That has never happened."

"But it might," said Barch.

"You think strange uncomfortable thoughts," said Kerbol.

On the following day the overcast was high, the wind light. The tribesmen hung close to the cave. But no bugling cries were heard and the Klau did not appear.

The next day was the same, with a near calm across the valley. Again the men of the tribe ventured only a few hundred yards from the cliff, and at the evening meal there was only a few scrapings of gruel in the pot.

The third day dawned blustery, with ragged gray clouds breaking over Mount Kebali like surf over a sea-wall.

Clet ordered Flatface, Barch, the Modoks and the Calbyssinians out to grub for meal-nuts, while the remaining men filed into the forest to hunt meat.

The bugling of the Podruods sounded an hour later. Barch and the Calbyssinians jumped up, seized the half-filled bags, hurried back around the hillside.

Across the valley rang the hunting cries, converging near the dominating bluff; looking over his shoulder Barch glimpsed the ominous dark shadow of the Klau raft.

The hunters came filing back to the cave one at a time, wide-eyed with exhaustion.

Across the valley the bugle-calls suddenly ceased. Standing in the crevice Barch saw the black raft slipping down the valley toward the notch.

Four hunters had not yet returned: Clet, Moranko, the two Splangs, Chevrr and Skurr.

Clet slipped in first, his bony red face impassive. Then came Moranko carrying a dead creature that looked like a woolly caterpillar.

Minutes passed. Chevrr crossed the flat. He muttered a few words to Clet, jerked his thumb across the valley.

Skurr, the Splang, had been hunted down and killed.

On sudden impulse Barch dropped into the seat opposite to where Clet sat whetting his knife. "I think we should do something about these hunts."

Clet turned him a brief cool glance, returned to his work. Steel rasped on stone, lamplight flickered and winked on the metal as the big red hands methodically stroked. Barch raised his voice. "We don't necessarily need to skulk around this valley." He paused; Clet showed no interest.

Trying to keep anger out of his voice, Barch said, "Every week somebody else gets killed."

"More always come," said Clet. "Too many in the cave is not good."

"Next time the Klau hunt, they might get you — or me." Clet shrugged. "We should hunt them instead — kill the Podruods, kill the Klau."

"No, no," said Clet impatiently. "Then a warship comes down to kill us all. We live good now, hey?" He laughed complacently. "Food, women, hey? Same way for many, many years. Best not to change."

Barch rose slowly to his feet, staring in frustration down at Clet, who glanced up impassively, then returned to his whetstone.

Five days passed, low angry days full of rain and stormy gusts that filled Big Hole with eery whistling sounds.

CHAPTER XIII

THE SIXTH DAY WAS QUIET, with a high overcast rippled with fish-scale black. Barch sought Clet out at where he ate his breakfast of toasted meat and gruel-cake. "Today the Klau might come again. If we went down to the notch, and hid where they enter the valley —"

Clet shook his head stubbornly, at the same time gnawing a bone.

Komeitk Lelianr knelt by the fire, tending the gruel-cakes which baked on a hot rock. She turned her head, spoke shortly. "Don't argue with him, Roy, he's very single-minded."

Clet looked up. "What does she say?" He dropped the bone, put his wide red hands on the table.

Barch looked down at him in disgust. Blood raced through his body. He felt strong. Perhaps his wind was better. His voice came out harsh and deep. "Maybe you want to live in a cave all your life like an animal."

Clet's eyes gleamed under the black eyebrows; he seemed to be listening not to Barch so much as to an inner secret voice.

"There's ways of leaving Magarak, if we'd work together."

Clet grunted contemptuously, turned back to his bone. "Now comes the crazy talk."

Barch was taken aback. "Crazy talk?"

Clet's big white teeth glittered in a grin. He flourished the bone toward Komeitk Lelianr. Barch followed the gesture in puzzlement, then suddenly understood.

Komeitk Lelianr pensively prodded the gruel cakes.

"She told me much about you," said Clet. "You are a crazy man; you would fly through space like a magician." His voice rose, his eyes glittered. "Now, no more crazy talk; this is Palkwarkz Ztvo, I am Clet."

Barch slowly went to the mouth of the cave, he took his bow and quiver of arrows.

"Ho!" Clet called out gruffly. "Where do you go?"

"None of your damn business."

Behind came the sudden scrape of the bench; Barch saw Clet reaching for his own bow. He ducked out the cave mouth, ran across the open space. He glimpsed Clet standing in the crevice like a heroic statue of Mars: bow bent, arrow tense with imminent mission. Barch flung himself to the ground; the arrow sang over his head. He rose, dodged into the trees where he pulled an arrow into his own bow, waited, pale and shaking.

After a careless survey of the valley, Clet returned inside the cave.

Barch walked morosely down-slope under the flapping fronds. An inglorious exit, he thought. He stopped, looked back toward the cave. He recalled the first time he had seen Komeitk Lelianr, stepping jauntily from the circus-striped space-ball. If she had noticed him at all, it had been as part of the local scene, a native. He felt a sudden glimmer of insight into her mind. Poor devil, thought Barch, she even found Earth food revolting...Well, that was all water under the bridge. And now what? Probably, after Clet's temper had run its course, he could return to the cave. And so the years would pass, while he grew older and his fire died out.

No, said Barch, not if he died today under the Klau raft. He turned, ran at a half-trot to the notch at the valley mouth. He climbed the left-hand slope, settled himself at the narrowest spot.

Time passed. Wind blew chill down the valley, a rim of black clouds loomed past Mount Kebali. A drop touched his nose; only one. The rain hung off in indecision. A poor day to expect the Klau.

He heard the scrape of boots on rock, the soft clang of Podruod voices. Barch tingled with primeval emotion. He sat up straighter, eased his muscles.

Into the valley eight Podruods came trotting, light as dancers in their black boots. Cuirasses covered their chests, black hair-spikes vibrated with each step. A cushioned raft followed, floating three feet off the ground. A young Klau in maroon harness sat fingering a pair of weapons on a rack. He halted the raft, glanced easily around the valley. Barch glimpsed the blood-red stars in his eyes.

The Klau touched controls with his feet, jumped to the ground, stretched. Negligently he conferred with the Podruod sergeant, studied the contours of the valley, pointed.

Six Podruods moved quietly off into the black fronds, two remained behind, squatting a little distance up the valley.

The Klau languidly took one of his weapons — it looked much like a long-barrelled automatic, thought Barch — balanced it in his hand.

Barch eased himself into position. He stretched the bow...Now! The arrow hummed down, plunged into the back of the black head.

Barch crashed down the slope, sprang to the raft, reached across the black body, seized the weapons.

The Podruods said "Oh!" — a soft hiss of outrage and horror.

Barch aimed, pressed the trigger. Nothing. The Podruods loped forward, mouths open in contortions of great rage. Barch clawed at a lever, perhaps a safety lock. He pressed the trigger, the first sprawled on his face. Barch pressed again; the second fell.

Barch listened. Silence except for the murmur of the river, a distant sound of snapping foliage. Now what? He seized the Klau's maroon harness, dragged the body into the undergrowth. He returned to the raft, seated himself; it bounced like a boat under his weight. He put his feet into the controls, experimented.

The raft shook, dodged back and forth, rose up an alarming slant. Barch pulled away his feet; the raft sank slowly. Once more he tried, and presently brought the raft back to the mouth of the valley.

He jumped to the ground, inspected the horrid black bundle under the raft. He took a knife from one of the Podruods, cut at the two bands which held the thing against the raft. It fell to the ground with a sodden spongy sound. Barch gave it a cautious kick, rolled it over, down into the river, where it expanded, opened, lay flaccid.

The next problem was how to deal with the six Podruods still in the valley. He rode the raft up the wall of the notch, settled where he had kept his original vigil. He waited an hour with complete patience. The wind had lost its bite, the sky was high and mild.

A quarter mile up the valley he saw the Podruods, apparently confused by the Klau's ineptitude. Barch laughed quietly. A few minutes later they came diffidently along the valley floor. At the Podruod corpses below him, they stopped in great puzzlement, looking in all directions. Barch aimed, fired swiftly six times. Six men fell as if playing a nursery game.

Barch descended, dragged the bodies into the foliage. The next hunting party might or might not notice the odor of carrion; at the moment Barch did not care especially.

He climbed aboard the raft, flew low over the tree-tops up the valley. A hundred yards from the cave he moored the raft, jumped to the ground. Cautiously he approached the crevice. One of the Modok women, fetching water, looked up without interest. Barch nodded to Kerbol who sat outside scraping at a bow, entered the cave.

Clet looked negligently up from the table. "Here is the crazy man, back from his hunting." He put his big red hands flat on the table, started to rise.

Barch lifted the gun, pressed the trigger. Clet fell forward. Tough on Clet.

Women were screaming in surprise and terror; Flatface bellowed in outrage; after a quick look the Modoks darted white-faced from the hall. Barch said in a voice as casual as he could contrive, "Call everybody in here. I'm running this outfit now and I've got something to say."

Chapter XIV

The cave gradually filled with whispering figures. Barch sat on the table, with his feet on the bench. He looked around the cave. Thirty-two in the tribe with Clet and Skurr dead.

He considered what he had to say — a problem in polemics that would daunt anyone. Thirteen different races, thirty-one different brains; thirteen basic mental patterns, thirty-one sub-varieties. An idea which aroused one would leave another indifferent.

The Modoks had no concept of individualism; Moses had been born into a world of absolute anarchy. Flatface bred his two bald harridans without restraint; the Calbyssinians ached for their perfumed nuptiarii and the anonymity of darkness. The Byathids avidly ate gruel and meat; Komeitk Lelianr swallowed each mouthful with an effort. Kerbol sweated; Chevrr shivered.

Each mind reacted to its own set of push-buttons; each mind languished in its private kind of inertia. There was no universal catalyst to excite each of the minds, and he certainly could not hope to infect each with his own Earth-type drive. At best he could goad them into action by vigorous leadership. At worst he could rely on the authority of the Klau weapons, and never allow a man behind his back.

He considered the faces around the hall. Lamplight flickered on skins of many colors, reflected from anxious eyes. This was a crazy man, who seemed careless with the death he carried in his hand.

"One thing is important," said Barch, "I did not kill Clet because I hated him. Clet is dead because he was stupid. Clet had to die because he had the mind of a slave. Under Clet you slunk around the hills like animals. The Klau came each week; each week someone was hunted along the valley and killed. In not too many weeks everyone here might expect so to be hunted to death.

"Now, there will be a difference. We are no longer slaves, we are men. When the Podruods come into the valley we will kill them. There is no need to run. We have bows, we have arrows, we will kill."

"Hah!" The exhalation came from one of the Griffits, who stood twirling his little whiskers.

"But this is only incidental. The main thing is escape. I want to leave Magarak. I want to return home. You others, do you wish for your homes?"

There was a mutter of low voices.

"Who says it cannot be done, if we give ourselves entirely?"

Kerbol rumbled stolidly, "You speak wild words. We cannot fly space like moon-dragons."

"There is no way," bawled Flatface.

"Both of you are wrong," said Barch politely. "A few months ago a dozen Lenape escaped. There are a hundred ways. This is my idea." He paused. There was complete silence. "We will steal a barge, build an airtight compartment upon it. We will load on food and stores, and leave Magarak behind us. The plan is as simple as that. There are difficulties; they must be overcome. The plan is not impossible. We have nothing to lose; are we not already condemned to death by the Klau?

"When we leave Magarak, we will fly for the nearest friendly planet. We will be a long time in space; eventually we will arrive. But from the moment we leave Magarak, we are no longer slaves, or fugitives; we are space-travelers. And when we arrive, we will be heroes, and we will have much to tell our friends and our families."

Once more he looked around the circle of faces. How could they help but alight to his enthusiasm? They must be as eager as he to leave Magarak.

Chevrr, the hatchet-faced Splang, snapped, "Talk is easy. Where will we find this barge? Where will we find materials and tools?"

Barch laughed. "Those are the problems which lie ahead of us. There will be many problems; there will be much work and danger. But if things go well, we will win. What do we have to lose? By acting instead of existing, we stop being animals; we become men."

"Where can we work on such a barge?" came Kerbol's bass rumble. "It will be seen from the air. The Klau will land a crew and fly it away."

"One place I know of," said Barch, "is Big Hole. The outside wall is a shell; light comes in through fissures. We will break an opening, slide the barge through, then pile rock back up... Now what do you say? I cannot build a space-ship alone; are you with me?"

Looking around the faces, he saw passivity, confusion, stupidity. He also saw here and there glimmerings of hope, imagination, enthusiasm. His eyes met Komeitk Lelianr's, where she stood by the wall, a pale golden figure, silent, disassociated.

Kerbol rumbled, "It is worth trying. We lose nothing. We will try."

"Good," said Barch with a tight smile. "I see you are all with me. But in case —" he looked casually down at the sprawled red body of Clet "— any others think like Clet, now they should speak."

No one spoke.

"Excellent," said Barch with a rather broader smile. He jumped down to the floor. "First things first. Before we liberate a barge we need a place to hide it."

He took up a lamp, climbed the passage into Big Hole. The tribe hesitated, then one by one followed.

Damp gray walls glistened in the yellow light; shadows sagged and danced. Where the passage came up from the hall, the floor was almost level in an area a hundred feet square. Ridges of agate jutted up at the opposite end, where the wall was thin.

Barch crossed to the far wall, climbed up the loose detritus. "Here is where we'll open out. Quite a job but it's got to be done."

Kerbol grunted. "With a few cans of abiloid I could blast a hole as easy as husking a nut."

Barch considered him thoughtfully. "You worked at the stone quarry over the hill."

"Five long years."

"You know where they keep the explosives?"

Kerbol grunted.

"Tonight," said Barch, "you and I'll visit the stone quarry."

✳

Night had filled Palkwarkz Ztvo for two hours when Barch and Kerbol climbed aboard the Klau raft. Mist blew on their faces as the raft rose; the mountain-side below was featureless as crumpled black cloth, except for a single spark of light, winking on the flat before the cave.

Kerbol touched Barch's arm. "Over there, up over Mount Kebali; then down."

Barch nodded. The raft drifted up into a region of fog. Mount Kebali loomed ahead like an underwater reef; they crossed fifty feet over the scoured rocks.

Down on the slope appeared a lonesome cluster of lights, far beyond lay the luminous blur that was Quodaras District.

"Kerbol," said Barch to the dark shape behind him, "in this project we've got to trust each other like brothers — and also take sensible precautions. What, in your opinion, are the chances of someone in the tribe betraying us to the Klau?"

Kerbol made a rumbling sound. "The chances are nonexistent. The traitor would gain nothing. The Klau would not take such a crazy tale seriously —"

"Mmph," said Barch.

"— The tale-bearer would be sent to the arsenic mines as an escaped slave. True," he went on, "there are some with small urge to leave Palkwarkz Ztvo; life on their home worlds is no better. On the other hand, some highly-ranked planets are represented in the tribe — my own, Perdu, Calbys, Koethena, Lekthwa." He paused. Barch said nothing.

Kerbol spoke on, "I will be glad to see my home village; it lies in the plain of Sponis, which is blue with turf and runner lichen, and there runs the river Erth."

"Earth?" said Barch. "That is the name of my planet."

"Earth?" Kerbol rolled the word on his tongue. "I have never heard of it." He ruminated a moment. "You must be wild and fanciful dreamers on Earth. I have slaved twelve years on Magarak, lived a free man in Palkwarkz Ztvo for two; never have I known anything so daring."

"It seems to me the first thing a man would think of."

The lights of the quarry shifted, spread slowly apart like the opening of a marvellous bright night-flower. The sight awoke in Barch the dream-end of a recollection. Where had he known another such opening-out of lights?

He sighed. Magarak night suddenly seemed harsh and bitter. Long long ago he had dropped Markel's air-boat toward a little village to buy lipstick for Komeitk Lelianr. He looked down at the stone quarry. "They must work all night."

"The quotas are hard; much stone goes for ocean reclamation. Notice," Kerbol pointed, "that north face is next on schedule; they drill now for blasting. And there —" once more he pointed "— is the explosives depot. The barge comes loaded, slides into the depot; empty, it slides out, and in slides a new load."

"And what precautions are taken?"

Kerbol shrugged. "First, an electrified fence which we will fly over. If there are alarm lines, we will avoid them also. Inside the warehouse will be a few Podruods, gaming or asleep, Bornghalese dispatchers who load orders onto an outgoing belt."

"We'll take them as they come."

The raft dropped, the quarry lights expanded. Ticking of hammers, intermittent grate of machinery came loud across the damp night. Bright blue points of fire showed where torches melted blast-pockets into rock. On the roof of the warehouse were outlined four dull squares of light — ventilation cupolas.

Barch lowered the raft to the roof, stepped off, walked carefully to a cupola. He eased his head into the light, looked down. He felt a tread behind him: Kerbol. Barch said, "There's nothing here! The place is clean, empty."

Kerbol bent his head. "True," he muttered. "There's not even a sack of blow-powder." He straightened, looked at the rock face a half-mile away, then bent his head over the ventilator again. "Even the barge is gone."

Barch eyed the sky. "How soon will new supplies get here?"

Kerbol shrugged. "Tomorrow, tonight…"

"Look," said Barch, "those red lights."

"That's the new load."

"Come on," said Barch. He sprinted to the raft.

"What now?" asked Kerbol, as Barch swung the raft into the air.

"Maybe we'll get more done tonight than we bargained for." He pushed the speed pedal down hard, swept out wide, circled, approached the barge from the stern. "Where's the pilot?"

Kerbol pointed. "In the dome at the prow."

"Be ready with your gun." He skimmed in over the barge, dropped to the deck. "I'll take the pilot, you handle the rest of the ship." He ran stealthily forward; the pilot was a sharp-featured silhouette, eyes on the lighted rectangle of the warehouse. Barch wrenched open the door to the dome.

"Take the barge up...Up, quick!" He pointed the gun. The pilot, a beady-eyed little man with a thin dark face cast a startled look over his shoulder. Barch said, "Quick — up!"

The pilot turned reluctantly to the controls. "I must follow my schedule, or the dispatcher will —"

"You're a dead man," growled Barch, "unless we're moving up right now!" He jabbed hard with the gun barrel. "Up!"

"We're going up!" said the pilot peevishly.

"Faster!" Barch looked over the side. "Now, back the way you came."

The barge swept away from the quarry. "Now — out with those side-lights," said Barch.

"I'm not allowed to," protested the pilot. "It's a punishable offense."

Barch grinned, tapped him on the back of the skull with the gun barrel. "Out with the lights!" He looked quickly over his shoulder. "Any crew aboard?"

"No crew. I load at Phrax District Chemical Complex, discharge at the warehouse."

"What's your cargo?"

"Explosives, general supplies."

Barch heard footsteps; Kerbol looked in.

"All in order?"

"Nobody aboard."

"Good." Barch backed out of the dome, motioned Kerbol in. "You steer him, you know the lay of the land."

Barch went over by the edge of the barge, looked out into the darkness. Step one. Achievement. He felt the bulwark — chill hard metal, the same hard metal which one day would lift him clear of Magarak out into great space.

CHAPTER XV

THE BARGE SLID UP the slopes of Mount Kebali. The sounds of the quarry faded; the lights contracted to a tight cluster. The sea of trembling luminescence, the factories, furnaces, mills and yards of Quodaras District now lay astern.

Barch took a proprietary stroll around the deck. It was rectangular, eighty feet long, fifty feet wide; the cargo was stacked ten feet high — surely not all explosives. Even on an Earthly scope, here was enough potential to pulverize half Mount Kebali.

He circled the cat-walk, looked into the dome. "Faster." The barge lurched under his feet; he staggered back into the cargo. The craft had quite a power-plant, he thought — all to the good if ever they reached space.

Moisture suddenly sprayed his face; they were driving through fine rain. He stumbled up into the lee of the dome.

The rain stopped, the barge broke out of the mist into a biting wind. Barch noticed the pilot's head suddenly twist. Turning, he saw the running-lights of another barge at their left hand. He walked to the rail with his gun ready...The barge drifted across their bow, disappeared into the cloud bank.

Palkwarkz Ztvo lay below, a dark wilderness. Barch strained his eyes for the wan flicker of light. Like a faint star at the horizon, it eluded him. He put his head into the dome, asked Kerbol, "Can you see our light?"

Kerbol pointed. "There." He nudged the pilot. "Land beside that light."

"Impossible," muttered the pilot. "We are over Palkwarkz Ztvo — wild-man country. They'll put us in their pots."

"No, they won't," said Barch. "Land beside the light."

The barge sank. Blackness blacker than the sky reached up past them; there was a crash, a snapping of foliage. The raft touched ground.

Barch looked warily out into the darkness. All was quiet. He turned to the pilot. "Get out."

The pilot hesitated, clinging to the protection of his dome. "What are you going to do with me?"

"Nothing."

The pilot jumped, made a quick dash for the underbrush. Barch tackled him around the knees; both fell into the soggy humus. Barch rose, seized the man by the collar of his jacket, marched him back past the barge, up the slope. Kerbol came after like a stealthy gray bear.

Barch entered the hall with the pilot. The entire tribe was huddled around the great table talking heatedly; Barch stood watching the play of firelight on the unearthly features.

There was a hiss, the talk halted; faces swung around as if operated by a lever.

Barch gave the pilot to Kerbol. "Lower him into one of the potholes on a rope." He turned back to the big table. "We've two or three hours work outside. Let's get it over with. Bring out your knives and axes."

There was uneasy movement, slow uncomfortable rising to the feet. Barch watched impassively.

Flatface said in a surly voice, "Work is for daytime. This is night. Let the work wait." The others watched anxiously, poised and uncertain as rabbits.

This was the first test, the most important. Barch made no sudden move. He waited, let the suspense build up. Flatface nervously glanced at Barch's gun. Barch said softly, "Where is your axe, Flatface?"

Flatface motioned to the wall. "There it lies."

"Get it!"

Flatface slowly gained his feet. Barch jumped two quick steps forward. There was a startled swaying back. "Everybody! Outside!" He took the two lamps, went to the entrance, waited while the tribesmen filed out past him.

In the lamplight the barge was a large dark shape, vastly more impressive than words Barch could have used inside the cave. "There's your space-ship."

The tribesmen muttered with awe, excitement.

"Tomorrow we'll unload the cargo, but tonight we've got to cover it over with branches so it can't be seen from above."

Barch pulled himself up from his couch with the first glimmer of light. He pulled on the Modok smock, more threadbare than ever after repeated scrubbings with wood-ash, went out to inspect the barge. It seemed to fill half the flat, like a whale in the front yard.

To check the camouflage he mounted the raft, floated up into the sky. The forest was a matted black tangle, the barge an extension of the same tangle. Satisfied, he dropped back to the ground.

It was not improbable that the Klau would catch wind of their plans, with subsequent violent reaction. What weapons might they bring to bear? A bomb would do little more than splinter the mountain-side. Torpedoes against the side of the cliff would have greater effect. There was poison gas, flame, disease, all the conventional Earth weapons, and Klau weapons he knew nothing of. Barch could not talk away a peculiar sense of futility. Any serious effort would surely destroy them.

It was essential that the Klau remained ignorant of his plans. He must avoid giving them provocation. In one sense, killing the Klau yesterday was a mistake. But it had been necessary — an act which had given him an aura of power that killing Clet ten times would have failed to do. In the future he might have to back down on some of his fire-eating threats. Avoid the Podruods as best as possible; fight if cornered.

He circled the barge. The seamless hull rose four feet over his head. He tried to visualize a super-structure, and achieved only the picture of a deck-house on a sea-going freighter.

He climbed aboard. About half the cargo was crates of various sizes. Toward the bow lay four bundles of heavy pipe, a half-dozen mechanisms, apparently drill-torches, a dozen spools of smooth cable. A good haul, thought Barch. He revised his mental picture from a deck-house to a dome of air-tight fabric over the barge, held down against air-pressure by a net of cables.

He jumped to the ground, returned to the hall. Standing by the fire, he watched the women set out pots of gruel to boil. Komeitk Lelianr slipped into the hall from a crevice to the left. Clet's private chamber, which she had occupied the night before, lay off the passage down into the mountain. She met his eyes, looked away.

If only he could read her mind, thought Barch. He watched while she unobtrusively busied herself. The old pang which he thought he had put behind him, came stealing back to hurt his throat. He watched her more openly, and knew that she felt his scrutiny. If he wanted her again, she was his, by a kind of murky inevitable common-law.

Abruptly he turned his back, looked into the fire, torn by rising heats and emotions. The first time he had seen her, she represented a challenge; she challenged him now by her sheer presence. Then he had sought recognition for his race. Now the issue was personal. He turned his head, met her eyes again. What went on behind the quiet golden gaze?

Kerbol came blinking into the room, followed by the dour woman who was his mate. Barch felt a sudden sense of warmth, companionship. He had at least one friend in Palkwarkz Ztvo.

After breakfast he took Kerbol out to the barge, to inspect the cargo. Kerbol snapped open a crate marked with black and red symbols; inside were canisters the size of apples.

"Those are abiloid," said Kerbol, "a slow explosive. This —" he opened a smaller crate, which held dense semi-metallic bars supported on a red plastic rack "— is Super."

"Super — what?"

Kerbol shrugged. "Super is what they call it at the quarry. A small cut of Super is equal to ten crates of abiloid. But it's fast. It smashes. Abiloid pushes."

"I hope you can detonate them."

Kerbol picked out one of the cans of abiloid, touched a wisp of thread. "This is the three minute timer. To detonate the Super, you set it under a can of abiloid."

"It's all yours," said Barch. "There are your torches. Pick yourself a helper and open out Big Hole."

Barch returned to the cave, sent Flatface out in charge of a hunting crew.

At noon Kerbol reported the cave-wall ready for firing. Barch doubtfully eyed the sky. Fog was creeping down the slope of Mount Kebali.

"We'd better wait till dark. Then if any Klau fly over, the hole in the mountain won't hit them in the eye."

By mid-afternoon, the fog shrouded Palkwarkz Ztvo. Barch signalled Kerbol. "Set off your shots."

A few minutes later six blasts sent streamers of mist flying.

Barch entered the hall, took the down passage past Clet's old chamber, leaned over the glass-walled bubble at whose bottom sat the pilot. "Feel like working?"

The pilot looked up sullenly. "Kill me and have done."

"I don't want to kill you. I need your help. I wouldn't keep you in this hole if I thought you wouldn't run away."

The pilot's face became instantly cheerful. "I have nowhere to go; I cast my lot with yours."

Barch grinned. "That's a sensible decision, quickly arrived at." He lowered the rope, the pilot jerked himself up nimbly.

Barch took him to the barge, pointed to the gap into Big Hole. "I want the barge inside."

The pilot swung himself quickly into the dome. "The work of an instant."

Barch climbed aboard behind the pilot. "We'll fly in together."

"As you wish," said the pilot peevishly.

The barge rose off the ground, glided up the slope, inched inside the gap. Two fires burned on a level area at the far end. "Land between the two fires," said Barch.

The barge slid through dimness. Stalactites, stalagmites clicked and crashed to the floor.

The barge grounded. Barch saw Kerbol already had men at work piling rocks back into the opening. He turned to the pilot. "How is it that the Klau trust you with a barge? Aren't they afraid you'll escape to the hills?"

The pilot made a supple gesture. "What would I gain? We pilots live well. In the hills the wild men eat each other like garfish."

Barch forbore to challenge the statement. "What would happen if you went back now?"

"I would be discredited."

Barch studied the pilot's mercurial face. "I don't want to kill you," he said slowly.

"No of course not."

Barch ruminated further. "But I don't want the Klau to come looking for their barge."

"Far from likely."

"Unless you carried them tales."

The pilot blew out his cheeks. "My loyalty is yours forever."

"No one here but you knows how to pilot the barge. In a sense, you are essential to the success of our plan."

"And what is this plan?"

"There's no harm telling you. We'll build an air-tight hatch over the barge and leave Magarak."

"Ah." The pilot nodded. "Now, indeed, I will join you."

"Now? Your previous promises could not have been sincere."

"You misunderstand. We of Splang are very delicate in our meanings."

"Chevrr up there is a Splang; I have no difficulty understanding him."

The pilot hissed contemptuously. "He is the mountain stock, a crude uncouth race. We of the coast forests are a different people entirely."

"Well, no matter," said Barch. "I'll take a chance on you. What's your name?"

The pilot said something like, "T'ck-T'ck-T'ck."

"I'll call you Tick," said Barch. "You understand that I'll think poorly of any attempt to visit Quodaras?"

"Certainly. That's to be expected."

"Then help fill the hole with rock. I'll talk more to you later."

CHAPTER XVI

BARCH SAT STUDYING his list of the tribe members, a heterogeneous crew. There were the three Splangs, Tick, Chevrr, Chevrr's small dark woman; there was Kerbol and his dour gray mate; Flatface and his two quarreling bald half-breeds; the Calbyssinians, whose sex still remained mysterious; Pedratz, taffy-colored and smelling like a bull; Sl, the double-goer; Lkandeli Szet, the musician; the six silent Modoks; five Byathids; Moses, the dwarf; the handsome youth Moranko; the cat-like Griffits, who had silently asserted rights to the first two of Clet's women; there was himself and Komeitk Lelianr.

Of technical skills useful in the conversion of a cargo barge to a space-ship, there was a depressing paucity. Pedratz claimed a knowledge of welding; Kerbol displayed familiarity with explosives; Tick could fly the barge. But who knew anything about air purification, who could repair drive-circuits, who knew the lore of space navigation?

Barch, looking unseeingly into the fire, drumming his fingers, suddenly became aware of covert scrutiny, doubtful eyes. He stopped drumming, relaxed. Confidence bred confidence; be confident, Barch told himself. Be arrogant in your confidence. But confidence by itself would hardly produce the program which somehow he must evolve.

The first thing to do was isolate the problems, work on each by itself. First, there must be greater security against the Klau. Barch critically inspected the opening to the cave, where nothing prevented Podruods from stepping in to kill them all.

He rose to his feet, walked through the winding crevice out into the night. Darkness everywhere. The wind roared down the valley, the great black leaves flapped a melancholy undertone, like surf on a rocky beach. Behind him the faintest glimmer of light shone out the crevice.

Tomorrow he would arrange some kind of trip-alarm system around the clearing…There was still tonight. Barch returned within. Nearest the opening sat two Calbyssinians, Ardl and Arn busy at their incomprehensible love-making, each trying to divine the other's sex. Barch knelt beside them, took off his wrist-watch. "Tonight we keep guard. You two will watch first, for as long as it takes this little finger to move from here to here. Then one of you will wake —" he looked over his shoulder "— the two Griffits. Come outside and I will show you where you must station yourselves. It's important."

At the cave mouth he said, "Arn, you stand here; Ardl, you walk quietly through the forest at the edge of the clearing. At every circuit report to Arn. Change off if you like. When you wake the Griffits, give them the same instructions."

Returning inside he set four more watches, himself taking the middle watch with Kerbol.

One problem temporarily shoved back out of the way.

Tick, the hatchet-faced pilot, was engaged in conversation with Chevrr, his brittle country-man. Barch joined them. "Did you deliver freight to the quarry often?"

"Yes, I made the trip once every two weeks, sometimes oftener."

"But you took freight elsewhere?"

"Oh, indeed."

"How did you get your assignments? Did you work out of a central transportation depot?"

"Correct. My depot is — was — Quodaras Thirteen, and every day I might receive a different assignment."

"You must know Magarak well."

Tick preened himself. "As well as any man can know it."

"What if there was freight for a strange location?"

"There is always the locator in the dome."

"Locator?" Barch pricked up his ears. "A chart?"

Tick said with airy superiority, as if he himself had designed the mechanism, "No, no. Much more complicated and complete. It's a three-dimensional view-box, indexed to all parts of Magarak."

"Let's look at this locator."

Tick spoke volubly as they climbed the winding passage to Big Hole. "— A good barge, a fine sleek barge, fresh-fueled, and why? Because I, Tick, have done favors for Goleimpas Gstad, Dispatcher for Quodaras Thirteen: a Bornghalese, very influential. 'Tick,' says Gstad, 'the range of the hangar is yours; select a barge which reflects your own excellence.' So daily I watch the route-strip and only two days past comes a barge fresh from the growth-vats —"

"Growth-vats? Do they grow the barges, too?"

"Indeed." Tick turned Barch a look of surprise. "Do you not grow ships and vessels on your planet?"

"No," said Barch, "we use different methods."

"If you arrive home, as I confidently expect, you will be a great innovator. It is all a matter of selecting the correct secretors, of priming them with responsible fluids and directing the growth with care. As a result —" They rounded the sharp chunk of marble agate at the top of the passage, stepped out into Big Hole. Tick waved at the sleek black hulk silhouetted against the firelit limestone wall.

Barch stopped, impressed by the magnitude of his acquisition. "How do you refuel the barge?"

Tick made a disdainful gesture. "I am the pilot. I am never concerned with such matters... However, the *accr* is inserted in the hatch under the dome."

"How much? How often?"

Tick blocked a rectangle six by three inches in the air. "Once a month perhaps, a new charge is inserted."

Fuel shortage would be no problem, thought Barch. *Accr* was evidently an atomic fuel, compressed electricity, solidified radiation. It made no real difference so long as he could lay his hands on enough of it.

Tick sprang nimbly into the dome. Barch thought with a grim humor that if Tick ever made it into the trees, he'd be a hard man to catch. He followed more sedately. Tick was peering with interest into a glowing slit, a trifle to the left of the seat. "Ha, hm."

Barch waited impatiently. "Well?"

"Quodaras Thirteen is very active; I was watching the traffic."

"Let's see." Barch pressed Tick out of the way, looked inside the slit.

His first impression was of looking at a glowing, fleshy abstract painting. There were pink blocks, orange squares, feathery light-blue towers. Black lines webbed the pattern; almost invisible squares of white film floated above. Sparks of every conceivable color drifted slowly over the panorama. "Those sparks," asked Barch, "what are they? Barges?"

"Correct," said Tick cheerfully. "Each district has a distinct color; Quodaras Thirteen is pale green."

Barch said in a strained voice, "This barge shows as a green spark?"

Tick hesitated, as if troubled by a passing thought. "Well, yes."

"Show me on the chart."

Tick slowly twirled a knob, glanced into the slit. "There is Palkwarkz Ztvo. And there —"

Barch peered down at a pale gray physiographic outline of the mountains. A green spark showed dimly against the mountain-side.

Barch looked up quickly. Tick was sidling restlessly toward the door. "Come back here."

Tick crossed the dome with a cheerful expression on his face.

"How do you disconnect whatever is broadcasting our position?"

Tick's eyes wandered toward a little knob joined by a chain to the box. "Best not think of it."

Barch leapt forward like a leopard. Tick's eyes popped in alarm. "Disconnect that light, or I'll kill you right here!"

Tick babbled in a frenzy, "It's not allowed; Goleimpas Gstad would discredit me completely."

Barch tightened his fingers around the pipe-stem throat. Tick's eyeballs protruded an incredible distance. Barch released the pressure. "Disconnect that light!"

Tick, moaning and wheezing, bent over the box, tenderly broke the chain, slid back a plate, punched a glossy green bubble. "Gstad will reduce me to the manure belts."

Barch looked into the viewer. The pale-green spark had disappeared.

Barch turned back to Tick, who was feeling his neck. Tick said quickly, "There are other useful aspects to the locator. Observe. If I would return to Quodaras Thirteen Hangar, I find the name on this index..." He gave a rotary spindle a whirl, characters glowed and spun. "Then I touch this cell here —" he looked up plaintively as Barch grabbed his wrist.

Barch growled, "You don't seem to worry much about your life expectancy."

Tick made a chattering sound with his teeth. "A Splang Coaster defies death. The exact hour of his passing is chronicled at his birth in the beach sand. No act of God, Klau or man can mar the chart of his life."

"A good comfortable philosophy," said Barch without interest. He looked into the locator again. "I suppose every Klau on Magarak knows where the barge is by now?"

"Possibly, possibly not," said Tick. He pursed his lips thoughtfully. "It depends a great deal on how rapidly the lack of explosive at the quarry will be reported to the coordinator."

"And what's the coordinator?"

Tick said with an air of complete candor, "I don't know."

"What do you think it is?" asked Barch patiently.

"I assume it to be a mechanical brain, that notes and integrates apparently unrelated occurrences, calculates the most likely causes of effects and effects of causes."

"Oh," Barch nodded. "A kind of mechanical super-detective." He turned back to the locator. "Can this thing be detached? I'd like to take it down to the hall."

"Certainly, indeed." Tick sprang to the locator, snapped loose a pair of clips.

"I'll take it," said Barch. He motioned to the cave floor. "After you."

Tick jumped nimbly to the ground, started toward the passage down to the hall.

Barch said in a casual voice, "What's the hurry?"

Tick stopped short, turned Barch a quick smile. "None whatever."

Barch climbed to the floor with the locator under one arm, and ostentatiously hitched at the weapon in his belt. "Now we'll go down."

Chapter XVII

In the hall Barch set the locator on the table, went to look out into the night. Arn and Ardl, lounging close together, sprang apart with a guilty start. "Damn it," cried Barch, "if you can't stop love-making or whatever you call it long enough to stand watch, I'll strip you naked and then there'll be an end to this foolishness."

Ardl went smartly on his rounds. Barch turned to Arn. "Don't let that Splang pilot get past you."

"No, Roy."

Barch looked up into the sky. Suppose the position of the barge had been noted. If so, a barge-load of Podruod troops might drop down at any minute. He shrugged. If they came, they came. "Keep a good look-out, especially up into the sky."

Back in the hall, Tick was seated on the table, a hand placed proprietarily on the locator. "Many pilots fly dead; they set the cell, they sleep. Not I. I look at my locator —" he patted the box "— I fly with my hands." He held up his hands. The fingers ended in knobs, like a tree-toad's.

Barch saw Chevrr sitting in a corner watching scornfully. He crossed the room, squatted beside him. "Are all his race like him?"

Chevrr nodded dourly. "We stay in the mountains to avoid them. They breed twins once a year, they swarm in the trees, they are worthless except as acrobats and prostitutes."

"But how can I control him?"

"Kill him."

Barch grimaced. "I find killing hard to get used to. Besides he is the only one who can fly that barge."

The folds of Chevrr's gloomy face went through an amazing process of opening, smoothing, widening. Chevrr was smiling. "He wears a lucky charm; all coast-folk do. It is his birth sac, with the diagram of his beach-sands. You will find it inside a leech which sucks at his belly. Take this charm and you are his master."

"Ah," said Barch.

"Be careful. If he knows what you plan, he becomes a demon, a giant. No one in the room could hold him."

Barch stood up, went to Kerbol, spoke briefly, passed on to Flatface, then to Moranko.

Barch went to the table, moved the locator to the side of the room. Tick weighed no more than a hundred thirty pounds. He looked stringy and agile.

Kerbol and Flatface came up behind. Each seized an arm; Moranko grasped the spidery legs.

Tick looked up in sudden wonder. Barch stepped forward, pulled up the front of his yellow blouse.

Tick's eyes popped forward until more was out than in. He writhed his shoulders, Kerbol and Flatface were dragged half across the table. He tensed his legs; incredibly Moranko was jerked a foot from the floor.

There on the sweating writhing skin was a flat brown spot. Barch pulled it free with his fingernails. Two objects dropped to the stone floor of the cave: a metal locket and the leech which humped sluggishly toward the fire. Tick leaned down at the locket, his eyes protruded as if on stalks. He drew his arms forward; Flatface and Kerbol, panting and gasping, came across the table like pillows. Barch picked up the locket, snapped it open, drew out a wisp of membrane.

"Tick," said Barch, "sit still."

Tick's eyes receded into his head. Kerbol and Flatface gained their feet.

"Tick," said Barch, "will you behave?"

Tick sighed. "My life is no longer my own."

"Not one of us here owns his life. We're in this together; we'll leave Magarak together or we'll die together. Do you understand that?"

Tick made no answer. His eyes sought out Chevrr's, as if seeking sympathy.

Barch said, "Where I go, your charm goes. When we get free of Magarak, you'll have it back."

Tick said nothing.

Barch returned the locator to the table, looked in at the pulsing pastel landscape. "What are those transparent white squares?"

"I don't know," said Tick.

"What are the black lines?"

"Those are the underground belts."

"I see a bright orange spot with things like fish bones waving on top. How would I find out what place that is?"

Tick looked. "That's on the Ptrsfur Peninsula, Zcham District."

"How do you know?"

"The signs are on the strip at the top."

"And the orange block?"

Tick twisted a knob. A black dot moved across the panorama, centered on the orange block. Tick pointed to a line of glowing orange symbols on the cylinder at the side. "There you will read the function of the block."

Barch scrutinized the symbols. "Can you read them?"

"No."

Barch glanced around the room. Komeitk Lelianr sat looking into the fire watching scenes far across space. "Ellen, can you read this?"

Indifferently she came to look. "The manufacture of *padisks verktt*."

"And what is that?"

"*Padisks* is number nine in series ten — or eleven — of the artificial elements. *Verktt* are a kind of radiation valve."

Barch grunted. "Oh." He tentatively turned the dial again. "This thing should be a big help to us." He looked around. No one appeared to be excited. "It's a great piece of luck."

Flatface pressed his agate eyes against the slit, twisted the dial. "Ah — there is the Purpurat, where I wound bobbins four years."

Barch turned to Komeitk Lelianr, who seemed familiar, understandable — an illusion, he realized; in essence her mental make-up was as alien to his as that of Sl, the pale double-goer. "Tick told me about a Magarak coordinator — a calculating machine of some kind."

"Yes," said Komeitk Lelianr. "A manufacturing world is coordinated by what is called a 'brain' — a scheduling machine, which keeps the elements of the world running efficiently."

She twisted the locator dial, reading the characters. Barch watched a moment. "Ellen, it looks like you've got yourself a job."

She nodded without interest. Barch was fascinated by a new thought. "It means," he said somberly, "that we'll have to work together."

She inspected him with mild curiosity. "Why should we not?"

Barch flushed. The idea had seemed important. "No reason whatever." He glanced around the table to see if his discomfiture had been noticed. Eyes were on him; eyes black, blue, white, red, slate-green. He said gruffly to the hall at large, "We might as well talk this project over."

He waited, there was no reply. They were, perhaps, not accustomed to talking things over.

"We've got the barge," said Barch. "My idea was to fit on some kind of air-tight balloon, net it over with cable."

There was silence. Barch looked around the table. Moses, the dwarf, threw wood on the fire. Barch edgily said, "I don't see why it wouldn't work, but I'm no space-ship engineer. Maybe somebody has a better idea."

As soon as he spoke he felt more uncomfortable than ever — His voice had been querulous. A leader must be completely positive... But how, he asked himself, how to avoid the inevitable cross-balancing, the constant internal comparison of attributes and effectiveness when surrounded as he was by a dozen strange races? It was a constant challenge to measure up to the best of the universe... Barch sighed, gave up. This kind of thinking led to ulcers.

Komeitk Lelianr said off-handedly, "Far simpler to obtain another barge, and weld the two of them face to face."

Barch sat perfectly still a moment, to make sure of himself. "That sounds like a very good idea." He paused. "There's a point to consider. In space we'll depend on the lift units for propulsion, so that we can keep to our feet. I hope for at least one gravity constant acceleration, which will bring us to light-speed — or as close as possible — in somewhere near a year. After that — I don't know. Earth theoretical scientists are convinced that light-speed is the ultimate."

Komeitk Lelianr smiled faintly. "Earth scientists have little practical experience in space-travel."

Barch continued as if he had not heard. "The point I was trying to make was, if we carry the extra mass of a second barge, can we reach that acceleration?"

"Certainly. More easily than with only one barge. You will have available the lift of both barges; they work on a positive-negative principle, like electric-magnets."

Barch, a little at a loss, said, "Oh. I didn't know."

Pedratz, the taffy-colored, said, "Two coils of welding tape, two hours and two barges are one!"

Barch rose to his feet, walked outside to check on the Calbyssinians. Arn, standing alone by the doorway, gave him an aggrieved glance. Barch bent to look at the wrist-watch. "Your time's about up. I'll send out your relief."

He returned within, gave the Griffits instructions, went out with them, explained the wrist-watch, then came back to the table, with the feeling of returning into a chess match. He said, "Before we weld the barges together, it might be a good idea to deck over the first barge, with the effect of doubling our floor space. Also, we'd better install whatever machinery we need — the air conditioners, water condensers, the —"

Komeitk Lelianr said, "Lekthwans use a single unit, a sustenator. Carbon dioxide and water vapor are extracted from the air; water, oxygen are produced, as well as basic food-stuff. The Klau presumably employ something similar."

Barch wondered if she might be deliberately flaunting her superior knowledge. Probably not, he decided wearily; it wouldn't occur to her as desirable. He looked for Tick. "Hey, Tick — where do the Klau build space-ship sustenators?"

Tick came over to the Locator, twisted the knob. "That's the growing plant for the shell down there — the black and green. The final assembly is at Stalkoa-Skel, Magdkoa District, on the fourth tier. I once picked up a cargo for the space-works on Gdoa." He twisted the dial. "There, the red block."

CHAPTER XVIII

IT WOULD BE EASIER, thought Barch, if I weren't so darned nervous. He studied the rock-colored hulk to his right. Kerbol had no more nerves than a lizard. Ahead was the thin crouched back of Tick, piloting the raft, completely at ease, making a chirping cricket sound with his lips.

Barch looked back over the side. They flew low; under and among a stream of barges, cars, rafts, spheres and occasional flashing snapping objects like sheets of silver lightning. Overhead rose the massive sooty towers of Magarak, crowding the sky, crowding the imagination. Even higher, feathery trusses flickered back and forth; smoke boiled and drifted. Colored flares fumed and dazzled; the air rolled with sound: clanging, chugging, roaring, hissing.

On Earth, thought Barch, this would drive men crazy. Are Magarak workers sounder stuff? Perhaps it doesn't matter whether human brains hold out or not; perhaps labor is cheaper than sound-proofing.

Tick flew confidently, almost happily, as if he were in a favorite stamping-ground. Barch shook his head in wonder, giving grudging respect to a brain which so casually encompassed and accepted this appalling bedlam.

The raft halted. Tick gestured with a hand like a monkey-paw. "That's it." They hung over what appeared to be a funnel of concentric terraces, vast as a crater, shining with leaden rings of light. A great black building, diamond-shaped, hung precariously over the gap, the sharp corner reaching to the center. Pillars of green light, like thick neon-tubes, rose from each of the steps into the building.

Barch muttered, "Strange kind of factory."

The diamond-shaped building expanded, the funnel opened out like a target. "Hold it!" cried Barch. "Are you going to land on that roof?"

Tick waved his arm in a kind of lunatic light-hearted reassurance. "That's where the fulls come out; you want a full, don't you?"

"I want to see what we're getting into," said Barch. He clutched the handrail till his fingers ached. "The fulls come out? What does that mean?"

Tick patiently explained. "The in-barges drop into the pit, ride the slide-way; more than likely they bring a cargo of components which discharges into the storage bays. Then the barge climbs around inside the rings and the air-makers fall like plums into the hold. When the barge comes out at the top it is loaded tight... See! There it comes now!" Tick pointed triumphantly to a barge poking out an aperture of the diamond-shaped building, like a beetle testing the air.

"That's what we want," said Barch. "Drop down and be ready to land on the cargo as soon as it's safe."

"Safe?" Tick suddenly thought of his loss. "Nothing is safe, surety has fled; death rides one's shoulders like a brain-sucker." He turned to Barch. "Did you know that without the beach-diagram, a man may not even die properly?"

"Watch that barge," said Barch unfeelingly. "It's coming out."

The barge slid up into the air, round black bosses making a polka-dot pattern in the hold. "Hell and damnation!" said Barch. "Do they ship an army corps to guard the things?"

Kerbol squinted. "A dozen Lenape, six Bornghalese guards — worse than the Podruods."

Tick slanted down. "Tell me when to land."

Barch yelled, "Pull up, you idiot! We can't kill all those men!"

Tick turned the raft off to the side in injured silence. After a moment Barch said, "We'll have to wait for the next one... How long should that be?"

Tick waved his arm. "I have no knowledge. When I went up through the slide-ways on my barge, it took one hour, perhaps two. But we had better go back to the mountains; the project is impractical. Without my charm, I feel death close at my side."

"We don't go back till we get one or two of those sustenators. We can't breathe five years on a barge-load of air."

"But you do not attack," complained Tick. "The barge comes out, you draw back, you hesitate. Better to go back to Palkwarkz Ztvo and sleep."

"The next barge may have no guards on it."

"All sustenator barges carry guards. They watch the Lenape, who have grown and modulated the sustenators, and who go to fit them into the space-frame."

"Oh," said Barch.

Tick pointed. "Now here comes a barge to be loaded." He looked quickly at the locator. "Rust-orange — out of Mempas Six, a Bornghalese District. See, he brings crates of diaphragms and catalyzing filters."

Barch said, "Quick, board that barge."

"But we need no diaphragms, no filters. They are useless."

"By the time the barge comes back out, it'll be loaded with what we want. Sustenators and Lenape brains. Quick! Slide in close, where the pilot can't see." He looked over his shoulder. Rafts, barges, cars, ribbons of white energy, and above, the unbelievable silhouette of Magarak. A million men within half a mile, but no one would see.

Tick skidded the craft sidewise through the air; a trick Barch had never known the raft capable of. It flipped over the rail, settled to the floor of the hold.

Barch jumped off, onto the solidity of the barge. "Come along, Tick. Kerbol, slide the raft up under the forward apron."

Barch ran lightly forward, slid open the dome. The pilot was a graceful maroon creature, handsome as a hero's mask, but when he turned to look, Barch saw the four-point star in his eyes — Bornghalese. No occasion for delicacy. Barch shot, pushed Tick into the pilot's seat. "Take over. Fly the barge down to the slide-way, then stay put in the dome. *Don't come out, don't say anything!* When you get a full load, start out for Gdoa."

Tick nodded, reached down, detached the dead man's assignment card, fixed it to himself. The diamond-shaped building loomed close alongside, the great black wall coated with matt enamel, soft black as velvet.

Barch seized the dead Bornghalese, hesitated. If he dragged the body back into the hold, he might be seen from the black diamond-building.

"Kick him out," said Tick off-handedly. "Let him fall."

Why not? thought Barch. He opened the front portal, shoved, rolled; the maroon body flapped down through the shadows like a demon-bird.

Barch turned to give last instructions to Tick, thought better of it. No need to instruct Tick in brass: that was carrying coals to Newcastle. He hastened back into the hold. The forward cat-walk created a dark shelter, Kerbol had slid the raft below, raised it to press up against the overhead.

The ringed terraces of the great funnel surrounded them; oyster-light from the dim sky reflected back and forth, back and forth; there were no shadows, a cool watery peace. Overhead the diamond-building took a harsh black cut out of the sky.

Barch looked around the hold for a hiding place, and perforce came back to the apron under the forward cat-walk. Where was Kerbol? Barch crouched in sudden cat-like caution, slunk forward, gun in hand.

"Up here," rumbled a hoarse voice.

Barch ducked, looked up into the cross-bracing under the cat-walk. "Oh." He swung himself up alongside, peered out through the lattice of metal lath. "I hope this turns out to be a good idea."

The converging terraces hemmed them close, each fifty feet tall, eighty feet wide, with narrow prismatic panes running up the height of the wall.

The barge grounded on a yielding floor; there was cessation to the near-soundless hum of the motors. The barge gave a lurch, slid into a dark hole. Watching anxiously through the lattice, Barch saw the high narrow panes against the sky. His eyes became accustomed to the blurred gray light, but he could find nothing familiar in the lights and shadows, the twisted tubes, slantwise planes and curved surfaces opposite the window.

He heard voices. Four small gray men wearing dirty white trunks and clob-boots leapt down into the hold. From above dropped a tangle of black tubes. The gray men separated the tubes, touched each to a crate. The tubes coiled back on themselves, whisking away the crates. The little gray men followed. Half the cargo remained.

The barge floated along the slide-way. Lurid lights glowed on Barch's face; he turned his head, saw Kerbol huddled tightly in the corner as if impersonating a shadow.

A tall man yellow as a lemon, thin as a heron, wearing a conical green hat, stepped down into the barge, stalked thoughtfully back and forth, his eyes on the deck as if seeking a lost object. He bent, made a mark, stepped out with one stride of spidery leg.

The raft slid on. At one side gleamed the high prismatic panes, from the other came a soft hum with forms and shapes moving, twitching, jerking, contracting.

A musical horn blast sounded; a second spidery man stepped into the hold, walked peering back and forth. He bent over the first man's mark, straightened, looked up. A tremendous black shape dropped with frightening suddenness, buffeting the air three feet from Barch's face, cutting off his view.

A moment passed. The great black shape snapped away like the flick of an eyelid, and now the hold was clear except for litter.

The barge slid placidly, as if floating in a quiet canal. Voices receded into the distance.

New voices sounded; staccato, nasal speech, pitched in different tones. Barch perked up his ears; where had he heard such voices before? He craned his neck, glimpsed three figures bent over small carts. They had lank black hair, oil-black eyes, ivory-yellow skin, button noses. Barch's heart thumped: they looked like Chinese, they talked like Chinese...The raft slid on. The voices faded.

Peering through the cracks, Barch saw a low portal ahead. The barge passed through into darkness.

A tremendous hand seized Barch, banged him against the metal. A roar like a million whirlwinds rang in his ears. He seized the bracing, gripped for dear life against the pressure.

The barge slid into light. Barch unfolded his bruised body.

The hold was clean; the litter was gone to the last splinter. Barch looked across to Kerbol. "Are you still there?"

Kerbol grunted. Barch fitted himself gingerly back against the angle struts, which now seemed cunningly designed to press into his aches.

Two men with long pony-faces, mottled white and brown skins, wearing hats like mushrooms, hopped down into the hold, waited. They looked up, reached. A black case hanging on a tube, like a berry on a stalk, dropped into the hold. The piebald men shoved it into a corner; the stalk snapped away.

A minute passed, the raft drifted past a bank of blue, red and green lights. Then another sustenator dropped into the hold. Another rank of lights, another sustenator.

The struts ground into Barch's flesh, he shifted and twisted. Kerbol sat like a lump of putty, motionless. The hold gradually filled, the loaders backing stolidly toward the forward apron.

After an interminable period, the hold was full, except for a last row. The loaders climbed to the cat-walk, guided down the last eight sustenators from above, then jumped to the dock.

The barge slid on, around and up. Sudden vast bright space surrounded the barge. They had come out into a hall. The diamond-shaped building? Barch craned his neck, could see nothing but a high glowing ceiling.

He heard voices of a peculiar brazen timber that his skin recognized with instant contraction: Podruods. He saw massive red legs stalking around the cat-walk; he thought he heard Tick's light rhythmical intonations. A moment later the deck sounded to the thud of new feet. Barch glimpsed a round yellow-brown face. Greenish-yellow splotches like grease paint surrounded eyes like balls of opal.

One after another, perhaps a dozen, they jumped on rubbery legs into spaces between the sustenators, stood silent as bisque dolls.

Two Podruods went one to each of the rear corners, planted themselves like a pair of statues. The little round men looked up with the blank eyes of sheep.

Barch inspected them critically. Who were these? What would he do with them? They looked completely inept, useless — a burden to the tribe. He wanted brains; Lenape mechanics, technicians; what he got was little fat men.

Chapter XIX

GRAY DAYLIGHT POURED PAST the cat-walk into the hold. Barch heard the hiss of rain. A moment passed. Then the barge rose, headed out into the rain. The little round men slid behind the sustenators. The Podruods spat and blew.

Looking up into the stormy sky, Barch glimpsed the black shuttle of traffic. The struts pressed hard into his aching bones as the raft slid up on a slant. Barch eased his gun into position; he saw Kerbol follow suit.

They were flying in the stream of traffic. Barch could see nameless faces, pale splotches, peering blankly out into the rain. He should have instructed Tick to steer free of the lanes.

The barge slid along at a steady pace. A hull hung a hundred feet above, slightly ahead and to the side. Barch could see the propulsion mechanism, glass and metal viscera, intricate, vulnerable. He looked over his shoulder as if to convey his thoughts through the hull to Tick: go higher, go to the side, get clear.

The barge continued steadily. With a maddening sense of momentum and direction, Barch realized that Tick would obey him literally, fly to Gdoa. Rain slanted across the barge like strings of gray wool. Barch could see water trickling down the red skin of the Podruods. The spikes of black hair drooped, fell like sea-weed over the bull-shoulders.

The raft above slid sharply away. Barch squinted up into the sodden sky. So far as he could see — clear. He pushed the gun into the hold. "Wait!" muttered Kerbol.

A crystal-domed raft came darting overhead, hesitated like a hummingbird at a flower. Barch saw the maroon of Bornghalese skin. He glanced anxiously back to the Podruods; Kerbol's voice had sounded loud on his ears — but no, the hissing rain would drown out sound. The Bornghalese raft darted away.

Barch levelled the gun, glanced at Kerbol. Kerbol nodded. Barch pressed the trigger button. The Podruods dropped, one toppled over the side. Barch slipped down into the hold, stood bent nearly double from cramp and bone-ache. He hobbled out into the rain, looked up.

A Podruod loomed over him like a tower, but his gaze was toward the stern. Attracted by Barch's movement he looked down, opened his cavernous mouth. Barch fired. The body toppled at him like a falling statue. Barch ducked back, the body crumpled on the deck.

Barch swung to observe the little round men. They stood like a row of pumpkins, little round eyes staring.

Barch climbed cautiously up on the cat-walk. Kerbol was there already. He ran astern, took the Podruod serpent lashes. He peered over the side; the gigantic welter of Magarak pulsed, whirled, shuttled, gleamed. Barch decided against dumping the corpses. Somewhere was the coordinator, the Magarak Brain, fitting incoming data into patterns. If a piece was too big or too small or odd-shaped, it went to a special file. And presently a pattern might be made with the odd-shaped pieces. He slid the corpses into the hold, ran forward to the pilot dome. Tick was singing to himself in a peculiar falsetto whine, and at first paid Barch no heed.

Barch rapped the back of the narrow head. "Wake up."

Tick gave him a sad glance.

Barch went to the locator, reached under, snapped the chain as he had seen Tick do. "Now, how do you turn off the pointer light?"

"Push back the slide, break the bulb."

Barch did so. "Take us up into the clouds and head for home."

He went back aft, stood looking critically into the hold. The little fat men eyed him nervously. Barch growled under his breath. What to do with them? There was nothing he could do, except take them back to the cave.

He jumped down into the hold. "My name is Barch."

They looked at him solemnly. Barch said brusquely, "You're free men now; you're slaves no longer."

The little man closest to him asked anxiously, "How is this possible?"

"You have heard of the Palamkum?"

"The mountain where the wild men hide."

"That's where you're going now."

The little fat man shuffled nervously. "But why have you gone to such lengths for our benefit?"

"I haven't. I wanted a few of those sustenators. The only way I could get them was to steal the cargo. You happened to be aboard."

The entire group muttered together.

"Why do you want a sustenator?"

"Wait and see," said Barch shortly.

There was further muttering. "And what will become of us?" came the question.

Barch grinned in spite of his irritation; they were disarmingly like a dozen little pigs, little porkers fearful of the trip to market. "That all depends on whether the Klau catch us again. Right now you're escaped slaves."

Again they muttered among themselves. One jumped up on the cat-walk, ran to the pilot's dome. Barch followed curiously. The fat man looked in at the locator, glanced at the broken chain, then ignoring Barch ran briskly back to his fellows. Barch watched with puzzlement.

Kerbol muttered, "That's the worst about the Lenape; you can do nothing to their satisfaction."

Barch stared. "Are those Lenape?"

Kerbol grumbled and muttered.

Barch went slowly aft. He had visualized the Lenape as physically equivalent to their reputed mental ability.

In the hold the Lenape were talking heatedly all together; none heeded him. Where Barch before had imagined torpor in the opal eyes, now he thought to see depths of subtle wisdom. They noticed him; all fell silent. "You are Lenape?" asked Barch.

"We are Lenape."

"Then you understand something of how these things work?" Barch indicated the sustenators.

The Lenape seemed surprised, a ripple of expression passed around their faces. "Yes, of course."

"And if this barge broke down, you could fix it?"

There was a stir of amusement. "It depends a great deal on the extent of the damage, on the availability of replacement parts, tools."

Barch nodded. "Fine. Excellent."

They were passing over the sea and the mud-flats; the mountains of the Palamkum rose ahead, vague black objects swaddled and blurred in the mist.

Barch pointed. "That's your future home, until we convert a pair of barges to a space-ship and leave Magarak."

The Lenape listened blankly. The foremost said, "You think to fly space in a barge?"

"In two barges, face to face, welded together."

"Impossible."

Barch felt a sudden sinking of the diaphragm. "Why?"

"The Klau will never allow it."

"The Klau didn't allow me to steal this barge."

"The necessary components and accessories are numerous, hard to acquire."

"Like the sustenators? Like the two barges? Like the technical help? Like a secure place to work?"

"Exactly."

"All those we've got."

There was a moment's silence. Barch was the focus of a dozen curious stares. Then the first Lenape said, "A space voyage would be interminably long. The barges are insufficiently powered to generate second-order acceleration; you would float clumsily through first-order space, the deck pushing at your feet."

"Five years in space is no worse than five years on Magarak. At the end of five years we're home. And maybe you can work out some system to give us more speed."

The Lenape muttered nervously. "A grand concept. Is it practicable?"

Barch said angrily, "You don't act like you want to get home."

"No, no — Lenau is life to us!"

"A few months ago a dozen Lenape escaped Magarak."

"A simple affair for them; they merely bred a secret blister into the rind of the space-ship; that was all there was to it … None of this painful fitting and piecing and improvising."

"Any fool can shoot fish in a barrel." And Barch said in a disgusted voice, "Are you with me or not?"

The little round men muttered anxiously together, all speaking at once. Barch failed to understand how communication of any sort was possible. The foremost turned up his face. "We will work with you; there is no alternative."

Barch nodded in grim jocularity. "I thought you'd come around... Pass up those corpses; I'll drop them over the side now."

CHAPTER XX

THE NEXT DAY BARCH carried the locator back to the table in the hall, checked Palkwarkz Ztvo to assure himself that the two barges in Big Hole showed no tattle-tale sparks.

Four women came into the hall carrying baskets of gray truffles. One of them was Komeitk Lelianr. Barch studied her covertly. It came to him with a little shock of surprise that she had changed. This was no longer the Komeitk Lelianr he had seen stepping down to Markel's blue-glass terrace. Her youth, her pleasant girlish assurance had gone. He could not remember the last time he had seen her smile. She had lost weight, her cheeks were thinner, the sheen of her skin had dulled to a subdued old-gold texture.

She turned her head. For two or three seconds their glances held, and Barch felt a weighing, a calculation; her eyes seemed to see him for the first time as an individual.

"Ellen," said Barch, "I want to talk to you."

She came over to the bench. "Yes?"

"Sit down — over here, beside me."

She came around the bench, seated herself.

"Yesterday," said Barch, "I saw some Earth people — Chinese — among the slaves."

She looked at him thoughtfully. "Are you sure?"

"They looked like Chinese, they spoke like Chinese, they acted like Chinese."

Komeitk Lelianr chewed her lip. "It's certainly possible that the Klau are shipping in Earther slaves."

Barch gazed numbly at the fire. "That would mean the Klau have occupied Earth — killed people, destroyed cities."

She shrugged. "That is the usual pattern when they meet resistance."

"They met resistance all right."

She looked at him with her speculative expression. "Yes, knowing you I can believe it."

Barch suddenly realized that returning to the Earth of his memory was a hopeless dream. "And the Lekthwans? What of them?"

"Lekthwa and Klau have been enemies for thousands of years."

"But the Lekthwans won't help the Earthers get rid of the Klau?"

"Not by sending warships, if that's what you mean. We don't have the industrial resources. We have no Magaraks; no Purloppats; no Brengastels —"

"What are those last two?"

"Industrial worlds like this one, on the other side of the Klau rule."

Barch drummed the table-top. "I suppose there's no use borrowing trouble."

The head Lenape, whose name Barch had been unable to pronounce and had so called "Porridge", came into the hall carrying a sheet of parchment. He marched across the room, lay the sheet triumphantly before Barch. "This," he said, "represents the needs incident to any such project as you envision."

Barch stared at the meaningless symbols. "Is each one of these marks something you need?"

Porridge bounced up and down jubilantly. "Yes, if you remember, I was of the opinion yesterday that the project was unrealistic."

Barch said, "Let me have your pencil, whatever it was you wrote with." Porridge handed him a flexible fiber. "Now," said Barch, "what is this?" He pointed.

Porridge brushed the first division with his finger. "Lavatory equipment, with spares. Shielded running lights, automatic pilot, and star-finder, communication equipment —"

Barch sat listening in annoyance. Porridge continued reading in a voice full of gusto. "— This item is the pressure compensator."

Barch found it hard to speak. "Porridge," he said finally, "imagine us in space with nothing in the barge but the sustenator, which produces our food and water."

"Disagreeable," said Porridge.

"Would we survive?"

"The question of survival is not the point under discussion."

"Wrong. That's what I'm talking about. Every time I go out stealing things, I may or may not survive. And with me dead there's nobody else here with enough brains to get us off Magarak. So —" Barch scratched a cross through the first division "— out. Unnecessary. What is this?"

In a subdued voice Porridge said, "These are tools. Some I cannot translate, since they are very specialized. This is a hoist. This is a wire-splicer. These are various kinds of hammers, gauges, rotary buffers. All are quite necessary."

Barch sat back angrily. "What's wrong with you, Porridge? Do you think you're in a warehouse? We're out in the mountains. I thought you Lenape were intelligent people. Why don't you ask for cushioned work-benches, automatic power-drills?"

"We did," said Porridge. "Right there."

Barch snorted. "You're worse than the Lekthwans — you've got yourselves in a mental rut; you can't think anything but what some-one's thought for the last million years. Haven't you ever heard of the word *improvise*?"

Porridge screwed up his face.

"Buffer — what do you want a buffer for? Forget it! Hammers? Use a rock. Hoist? Run a sling under that little Klau raft." Barch crumpled the parchment in disgust. "I'll tell you what you're going to get: welding equipment, deck-plates, and fuel for the engines. We'll probably have another barge or two before we're done; you can strip it of any spare parts you need."

Porridge sat down heavily, kneaded his forehead. "You have a peculiar concept of comfortable space travel."

"I'm not interested in comfort; I want to get home."

Komeitk Lelianr said in a colorless voice, "Barch is from the planet Earth."

"Earth?"

"Out in Efrstl Region." Komeitk Lelianr looked at Barch dispassionately. "His people are socially disorganized, technically limited, ruled by emotion. But any kind of challenge seems to arouse in them a feverish energy. Barch thinks of it as *dynamism*. It is a necessity for action, no matter whether or not toward impossible ends. Rationality is a curiously ineffective argument against him; you are forced to think in his terms."

"Ah," said Porridge, and looked at Barch with new interest.

Barch smiled faintly. He said to Komeitk Lelianr, "You are still convinced that my ideas are impossible?"

Komeitk Lelianr stared into the fire. "No."

Barch relaxed. A significant victory. A great victory. He knew it, she knew it. "Now Porridge, I want you to be reasonable. I want you to exercise your brain. Be ingenious, clever. Tonight we're going out for welding equipment. If we see any tools we'll bring them along. Perhaps you'd like to come out with me?"

"No, no," said Porridge.

"You go back, start installing the sustenators, as many as the group of us will need. Also bring one or two down here, set it running; then we won't need to leave the cave for food, and we'll be safe from Klau hunters."

Porridge departed. Barch looked after him. He said to Komeitk Lelianr, "Whenever they get together they all talk at once. How do they understand each other?"

The spirit which for a moment had made Komeitk Lelianr's face bright and alive had gone. She said in the emotionless voice Barch had become accustomed to, "They speak and listen at the same time."

"All twelve? Twelve at once?"

"Yes."

"Mmph," said Barch, "that's remarkable."

She looked at him with a sidelong expression Barch as usual could not fathom. "A moment ago you compared the Lenape intellect unfavorably with the Lekthwan."

Barch looked at her in surprise. She spoke as if she were piqued. "I was admiring the Lenape technique, not their originality. I once saw a dog walk a tightrope holding an umbrella between his teeth. I also thought that was remarkable."

Komeitk Lelianr made no comment. Barch continued thoughtfully. "I can't understand how even a dozen of them managed to escape."

"It was a different situation. You judge them from the perspective of your own culture, your own experience — a narrow viewpoint. A fish cannot swim on dry land. This environment — here in the mountains — is one which gives your abilities full scope. In other situations you might not perform as well. The twelve Lenape who escaped fed extremely subtle mathematics into the breeding tanks. They performed well; they manipulated ideas and mechanisms they understood. The Lenape here are not in that position."

Barch digested the idea, and decided to discontinue the argument. "Perhaps you're right. Now to work. Where do we find welding material? And deck-plates?"

Komeitk Lelianr turned to the locator. "Sooner or later you will be captured and killed."

"That's undoubtedly true. Every time I go out my chances are about two in three, which is not too bad. Sooner or later I'll run into the third chance…Of course we have advantages; there's such a tremendous flow of traffic that it can't all be guarded."

"But the Brain knows."

"Yes," said Barch, "the Brain." He looked at the locator. "Possibly the Brain is indexed there?"

"Possibly."

"Do you think you could possibly find it?"

She shrugged. "I'll try." Tick came diffidently into the room. "Tick," called Barch, "come over here."

Tick sidled up to the bench without much enthusiasm.

Barch looked into his long sallow face. "What's the trouble?"

"I feel the pressure of my time. I sense the odor of death. If I once more owned the charm of my destiny, I would be secure when all else dissolves in fire and ruin."

Barch said thoughtfully, "From one point of view — yes. But the charm is surely as effective in my possession as it is in yours. Now sit down, and tell me the best place to steal welding supplies."

CHAPTER XXI

RAIN FELL INTO PALKWARKZ ZTVO, curtains and streamers gray as mourning crepe, hiding the twilight. The black mountain-side blurred and melted like dark sugar; black fronds pounded and dripped.

Barch, Tick and Kerbol had gone off in the raft an hour since. Lenape grouped at the far table, muttering excitedly, tapping the table with fluttery little fingers, from time to time referring to calculations on a sheet of parchment. Lkandeli Szet, the sad-eyed musician in the embroidered black and green smock, sat drawing plangent vibrations from his string-box; beside him squatted the Calbyssinians blowing windy organ notes through their fingers; Chevrr, the hatchet-faced Splang, crouched as near to the fire as possible, mending a tear in his leggings; the light made moving pools of black along his deep marked face. Flatface lay nude on the bench while his women massaged his back; over his head a listless dice game was in progress. Only Pedratz displayed excitement, and this because he read omens in the fall of the dice.

Komeitk Lelianr came quietly into the hall. She crossed to the entrance, wound through the S-shaped crevice, stood looking out into the rain. Darkness was absolute; there was nothing visible but the hissing vibration.

A step at her back: hard hands gripped her, forced her to the sand. This would be Moranko, who the last two days had been importunate. She relaxed, thinking it was easier to submit than to resist; then a sudden new idea intruded, and she curled into a ball, twisting away from the hot hands. She crawled down the passage with Moranko clutching at her ankles. A corner of rock scraped her side; sighing with pain she staggered to her feet, rounded the corner into the hall.

She went to sit on the bench beside the Lenape who paid her no heed. A moment later Moranko entered the hall, crossed the room and sat beside her. He bent, whispered in her ear.

"No," said Komeitk Lelianr.

He rose to his feet, petulantly struck her across the cheek. The Lenape turned their heads, inspected her owlishly, moved a little down the bench.

Komeitk Lelianr sat staring at the fire conscious of the pain on her cheek, the ache in her side, the new strange sensation inside her. There was sound at the entrance, she looked up. Roy could not have returned so soon.

She looked around the hall. Two big tables, benches, shadowy walls, crackling fire. Lenape arguing, chattering. Moranko's smouldering gaze. The plaintive sounds of Lkandeli Szet and the Calbyssinians. The smell of flesh and cooking and smoke. She closed her eyes. Outside were the dark mountains of Palkwarkz Ztvo and the black skies heavy as an ocean. This was her place until dying-time, unless — she looked up swiftly. The crevice was empty. And now she dared not go outside with Moranko watching like a dog watching meat.

Suppose Roy were killed tonight? Then she might despair indeed — even though she had never permitted herself hope. But Roy Barch worked, Roy Barch effectuated, Roy Barch brought the possibility of escape within mental grasp. With Roy Barch dead, life became stagnant, squalid, with this cave her life and her death. Her eyes grew moist; it came before her mind, suddenly large, that only the optimism of Roy Barch made Palkwarkz Ztvo bearable…A curious race, the Earthers. Young, only a few years removed from savagery, contaminated by the past, correspondingly exuberant and direct.

She considered Barch's word *dynamic*. Odd that he should feel the essential characteristic of his culture so clearly. She wondered briefly about Earth: had the Klau infested it wholly as they had half a dozen other worlds? Or did they merely maintain 'absorption centers' — depots for slave traffic? And what of Lekthwa? The longing grew too great, hope she could not allow herself; it would be self-torture even to encourage Roy. Hard on Roy, she thought. Roy gave the effort, the force; he was thanked by none. Barch, in the mind of the tribe, had become equivalent to hard work, when sitting beside the fire was easier, more pleasant.

An hour passed, during which the Lenape rose in a body, trooped into Clet's old chamber and carefully laid themselves down to sleep.

Another hour went. The fire flickered and lapsed to coals. Moranko still sat eyeing her darkly from the corner. He would wait till the hall was empty, then come for her. She looked around the hall. Flatface? Moses, the dwarf? Sl? Musky Pedratz? Whoever protected her acquired physical rights, by virtue of primeval law. Moranko was less repugnant than any to whom she could appeal, except possibly Roy Barch. It might be less taxing in the long run to submit once more to Roy Barch.

Flatface awoke from his doze on the bench, grunted, scratched himself, staggered off to his bed. Lkandeli Szet had disappeared. Armian and Ardl lay languidly twining each other's hair, while Arn blew soft chords through his fingers.

The coals grew dimmer, one of the lamps flickered out. Moranko slid to the bench beside her. "Come with me now or I will beat you."

Komeitk Lelianr listlessly arose from the bench. Moranko took her wrist, started to lead her from the hall.

Footsteps scraped and thudded in the entrance: Barch stood swaying in the entrance. Tick pushed past him, crouched by the fire. Barch's eyes swept the cave. "Where is everybody?" His voice was hoarse.

Komeitk Lelianr said, "They've gone to bed."

"Bed!" Barch's voice cracked with emotion. "They go to bed while..." He stopped.

"Roy," said Komeitk Lelianr, "what's wrong with your arm?" Barch was clutching the region of his left side in a peculiar manner.

He came forward, sank down on a bench, said breathlessly to Moranko, "Wake up the tribe. There's a barge outside. We've got to bury it into Big Hole."

"Roy," said Komeitk Lelianr, "your arm..." She felt suddenly weak in the knees.

"My arm and Kerbol," said Barch, "both back on the mud-flats." She saw he was crying, tears of grief and exhaustion. Carefully she pulled the bloody rags away from the stump, and went a little dizzy.

Faces peered over her shoulder, dull masks with eyes and nostrils wide, aroused to morbid excitement.

Barch said weakly, "Don't stand here; get to work. Chevrr! Where's Chevrr?"

"Here." The hatchet-faced Splang came out of the shadows.

"You know what to do…Open up the wall, slide the barge in, close it up again. Take over for me; I'm all in."

The hall was empty, except for Barch and Komeitk Lelianr. Barch lay on the bench, talking at random. "We've got it all — all in this load. Tools, welding tape, welder, deck sheeting…There were Bornghalese on the dam. We waited to throw in lights, portable lights. They came running."

"Lie still, Roy. Lie quiet."

"My left hand hurts — in the palm — and I don't have a left hand. It's mixed up in the mud with Kerbol…Oh, what a sight…"

Komeitk Lelianr tried to remember Lekthwan medicine, but the oddments and theories had no immediate bearing on a stump of an arm.

Pfluga, Flatface's second woman, too fat for work, came wheezing in to build up the fire. She peered at the arm. "And what will you do?" she asked Komeitk Lelianr.

"I don't know."

Pfluga snorted. "There's only the one way." She thrust a heavy poker into the coals.

Barch fainted, and when the smell of burning flesh reached her nostrils Komeitk Lelianr likewise fainted.

Pfluga snorted, sniffed, stirred the fire up under a pot of hot water. There would be calls for food and hot tea before the night was over.

The Lenape were dissatisfied; the tools were inefficient. Setting out across space in a pair of barges was like putting to sea on a log raft. Crude, intolerably clumsy and slow.

Barch lay back with his eyes shut, ignoring the patter of words. He heard Komeitk Lelianr hesitantly say, "The voyage is not impossible?"

"No, no, of course not. Impossible is the wrong word. Inadvisable, uncouth, indelicate. No bathing, no —" here the Lenape used a string of words Barch could not understand. He lay quietly listening.

Komeitk Lelianr said, "When you return once more to Lenau, these functions will again be applicable."

"True," said the Lenape. "But a year, two years locked in the barge with thirty ruffians?"

"Is it any more unbearable than living here in the cave?"

There was a flurry of words, the Lenape finally deciding that the space-voyage represented no greater hardships than continued life in Palkwarkz Ztvo, and so returned to Big Hole.

Barch opened his eyes, reached out to pull himself to a sitting position, fumbled ineffectually with the air. He realized that he no longer had a left arm, propped himself awkwardly with his right. He looked at his bandage. Clean gray cloth. The stump ached, not unbearably.

Komeitk Lelianr knelt beside him with a bowl of gruel. "How do you feel?"

"As well as could be expected…What's been happening?"

"You've been sleeping for two days."

"And what's been happening?"

"Three sustenators are welded in place. Today the decking is being put down. Tomorrow — well —"

"Two days." Barch rubbed his chin. "Two days…Help me up."

"You'd better sit still."

"I've got to think."

"Can't you think where you are?"

"The Bornghalese saw us up along the dam. They know a barge is stolen, they know what's aboard. When the Brain finds out…"

A sensation like a cold draught played along Komeitk Lelianr's skin. She glanced uneasily toward the crevice.

Barch asked feverishly, "Have you checked the locator index for the Brain?"

"It's not listed as the Brain," said Komeitk Lelianr uncertainly.

"I can't understand why they wait so long," fretted Barch. "It's unnatural."

Komeitk Lelianr said soothingly, "Another few days and we should be ready to leave."

"We need fuel — *accr*, Tick calls it."

"But — you can't go out stealing again."

"I'll have to. Who else will go?"

Komeitk Lelianr had no answer. After a while she said, "We'll also need raw materials for the sustenators."

"Raw materials?"

"Carbon-stuffs. The cycle inside the barge is subject to waste. The sustenators take carbon from the air and build food, but the carbon of excretory matter is ejected from the ship, lost. We need material to replace the drain."

Barch closed his eyes wearily. "There won't be a drain."

Komeitk Lelianr eyed him anxiously. "How is that possible?"

"Sewage is carbon, oxygen, hydrogen," said Barch. "Molecules don't get dirty."

"The concept is revolting."

"You'll get used to it. Qualms in Palkwarkz Ztvo are a luxury."

"And I suppose if someone dies, his body goes into the sustenator?"

Barch grinned. "In deference to your sensibilities, all corpses get a sea-burial. But if the Klau come first we'll all be corpses." He struggled to his feet. "I don't know why I should be so weak."

Komeitk Lelianr took his elbow, steadied him. "You've lost a lot of blood."

Barch winced, closed his eyes as if to shut out a terrible vision. He muttered, "That rascal Tick, hiding, dodging, slinking…If he had stayed where I put him —" he wiped at his forehead. "Well it's in the past; Kerbol's gone, the best man in the valley." Barch turned his glowing eyes full into hers. "He was loyal. Kerbol stood by his guns, even when he died for it."

CHAPTER XXII

SHE ABRUPTLY DROPPED his arm. Barch turned away, boiling inside with a hundred feverish rages and griefs. He made his way slowly up to Big Hole, where he leaned back against the wall, legs like wet rags. With gloomy satisfaction he listened to the sounds of activity. Barges 1 and 2 sat side by side on the flat, with the four floodlights that had cost so much blood hanging overhead. Barge 3 rested askew down at the far end, with the boxes, crates and miscellaneity of three cargoes in between.

Barch calculated up into the regions above. Stalactites glittered and twinkled; the ceiling was gloomy, complex, Gothic — but there seemed to be enough room, when the time came, to invert Barge 2 over Barge 1. A delicate maneuver, but Tick had a completely sure touch... As if Tick were telepathic, he looked up from where he squatted beside Pedratz, the welder, who was cutting pipe into stanchion lengths. He came bounding over the rocks like a cat. "Well?" asked Barch.

"When will you give me my charm?"

"You'll get it as soon as we're out in space."

Tick tugged desperately at his braided side-burn. "Too late, too late." His voice rose to a neighing. "I feel the bulk of terror, my brain aches, my knees are weak at wading through imagined blood."

Barch said in a cracked voice, "You'll ache all over if you don't stop that croaking. I've got your charm in my pocket; as long as I'm safe, it's safe. Think that over. Now go tell Porridge I want to talk to him."

Tick went crouch-backed across the stone floor; a moment later Porridge's round head pushed cautiously over the edge of Barge No. 1. The opal eyes fixed on Barch a ruminative ten seconds, then he climbed up to the cat-walk, backed down the ladder, trotted across the cave. "What do you want?"

"I want to talk with you about defending ourselves."

"I know nothing about fighting. The Podruods are the great fighters." He started to turn away.

"Just a moment," said Barch, grinning sourly. "We don't have any Podruods handy at the moment."

"True."

"From what you know of the Klau mind, how do you suppose they'll attack us?"

"I would assume that armored Podruod troops would be sent to kill us."

"And suppose that failed?"

Porridge's eyes bulged thoughtfully. "They might send a monitor with torpedoes to break open the mountain. Or they might establish a cone of lethal radiation against the cave opening and then we would be trapped like mice in a shoe."

"Come inside a minute," said Barch. "To send in troops, they have these alternatives. They can land a barge-load outside the valley, march them in, the same way the Klau come hunting. They can land a barge-load on this flat, in front of the cave. Or they can land them somewhere else in the valley which is unlikely, because there are no other flat landing-places within convenient distance."

Porridge looked uninterestedly along the damp black mountainside, then pointed across the valley. "A barge might land on the knoll of that bluff."

"Then the Podruods would have to climb down the steep slope and across those sharp rocks. However," said Barch, "that bluff would make a fine place to command the mouth of the cave. So that makes three areas we want to guard: the valley mouth, that bluff, and the flat here in front of the cave."

Porridge fidgeted. "Yes, yes. On Lenau we would convert the ground to a gel with vibrators."

"This happens to be the Palkwarkz Ztvo," said Barch. "I'm going to fly a load of explosive over to that bluff and bury a few mines. Can you build me a long-range detonator?"

"First, I must see the explosive."

"Let's go back to Big Hole," said Barch. He gave a last look up and down the valley. "A gray day; notice how high and thin the clouds are?" On a day like this he and Komeitk Lelianr had first dropped into the great sighing valley; on a day like this he had killed the Klau and liquidated Clet. "Klau come hunting on such days."

They returned to Big Hole, went to the crates taken from Barge No. 1. "Kerbol knew these explosives," said Barch, "I don't."

He pried open a crate, looked down at shiny gray bars lodged on a rack of rust-colored plastic. "This is Super. Very powerful. We've got about sixty crates. Enough to blow up half Magarak."

He found a second box. "This is the stuff Kerbol used — abiloid. And this string is the fuse, or detonator."

"Yes, yes," said Porridge. "Quite common."

"Can you work out a remote control?"

Porridge glanced down to the dome of Barge No. 2. "There are instruments which could easily be adapted."

"Good," said Barch. "Suppose you get at it right now."

"Very well."

Barch watched Porridge march briskly off. He felt eyes upon him — Tick's. When Barch turned his head, Tick looked away. Barch watched Pedratz the welder a moment.

Each length of pipe made one stanchion, with about five feet waste. The sight of the pile of five-foot lengths gave Barch an idea. He crossed the cave, tapped Pedratz's taffy-yellow shoulder. "Pedratz, seal off one end of about four of these." Barch pointed to the pipes.

Pedratz nodded, turned, prodded Tick with his toe. "Hoist four of those lengths into the dolly."

Barch's stump began to ache. He turned, left Big Hole, went down the passage into the hall.

He stopped short. From one of the dark alcoves came the sound of a muffled struggle, panting, gasping, a throaty growling. Barch swiftly crossed the room, hand on his gun. Komeitk Lelianr sat huddled against the wall, face dirty, hair in a tangle.

Moranko rose twistedly to his knees, to his feet. Blood trickled from his nostrils; his eyes showed white rings of passion and anger.

"What's going on?" asked Barch.

"I want this woman," said Moranko sullenly. "She belongs to nobody. Clet took her from you; Clet is dead, you have not taken her back. But she resists me; look, she has kicked my face."

Barch glanced down at Komeitk Lelianr who was combing her hair back from her face. His mind moved sluggishly among a hundred emotions. "The woman is no concern of mine."

Komeitk Lelianr's face never changed; she sat looking at him reflectively.

Barch turned sharply back to Moranko. "However, we are no longer a tribe of savages; we are civilized. If this woman wants to mate with you, good. If not, you must not force her."

Moranko's face went blood-shot. "She belongs to no one."

"She belongs to herself."

"It was not thus with Clet."

"Clet is dead." Barch turned to Komeitk Lelianr, who had gained her feet. "Do you want to mate with this man?"

She smiled faintly. "I have never wanted to mate with anyone."

Moranko turned, strode across the hall.

Barch turned back to Komeitk Lelianr. She opened her mouth as if to say something, hesitated. Barch waited. She said, "I am carrying your child."

Barch heard a droning in his ears. He looked in wonder down at the slight golden figure. A moment passed. He found his voice. "*My* child? How do you know it's my child?"

"Clet was a Podruod, one of the Klau sub-races, a different human species. There is no fertilization between his type and mine."

"Oh." Barch sat down at the table. "This is a new development." He looked at her a long moment. "And what do you expect me to do?"

She said listlessly, "Nothing. You did what I wanted when you sent Moranko away."

"And when this child comes — you will hate it?"

"No… It is not a child I wanted. But it is part of me."

Barch's mind raced across time and space. "And when we get back to civilization?"

"That is problematical."

"Yes," said Barch heavily, "and there is a great deal to be done."

He started back up the passage into Big Hole. In the dark something sprang ferociously at him, threw him to the ground. Barch fell on his stump, felt the flesh squash, the blood squirt, lay in a daze. He felt nimble hands at his pouch, a hiss. Then there was a kick at the nape of his neck, a scuffle of footsteps.

Barch lay quietly, doing nothing more than existing. After a moment, with a whirling head, he gained his knees; his thoughts began to assume form again...Moranko? A second idea brought him staggering to his feet. Or Tick? He clasped a hand into his pouch. No charm.

Barch ran limp-legged down into the hall. Komeitk Lelianr looked up at him in consternation. "Who came through here?" croaked Barch.

"Tick..."

Barch ran to the crevice. Tick would make instinctively for the raft. If he escaped, if he added his story to what the Magarak Brain already knew...Barch pulled out his gun. Tick was at the raft, tugging at the mooring line. He saw Barch, slid off into the forest, sprang into the trees like a monkey. Barch heard his shrill mocking laugh. "Too late, too late, you'll see me nevermore." And there was the rustle of branches, the clatter of black fronds.

Barch went to the raft, sank on it limply. He looked at the stump of his left arm; the gray cloth binding was sticky and dark. The bone ached intolerably.

He swung himself aboard the raft, untied the mooring line. Rising over the tree-tops, he coasted slanting down toward the river, the course Tick would presumably take. Underneath him the black fronds flapped and rasped, glistening like the scales of a great black fish. Tick was no more visible than if he had been an insect.

Barch lowered the raft to tree level, put his head over the side, listened. A soft crashing, not too far away. Barch manipulated the pedals; the raft slid like a shadow over the tree-tops. Barch stopped again. Silence. The sound might have been a wild animal. Directly below him Barch heard the crush of feet. He peered through the fronds, gun ready. But he saw not Tick but a Podruod.

Barch froze. The Podruod, walking as stealthily as his weight and the ground would allow, vanished.

Barch looked swiftly around the sky. Was this the Klau attack he had expected? Down toward the valley came a sharp hoarse cry, a high-pitched babble in a voice Barch recognized as Tick's. A vibrant bugle call. Below him heavy footsteps pounded, the Podruod running toward the sounds. Barch relaxed. A hunt, and Tick was the quarry. Best take the raft back to the cave before the Klau hunter rounded the bluff.

Barch slid the raft into its accustomed spot, sat listening. The Podruod bugle-calls sounded now up at the head of the valley. If Tick gained the wilderness of rocks at the foot of Mount Kebali, he stood a fair chance of escaping. But the trumpeting shifted, sounding ever louder. He's leading them to the cave, thought Barch. He limped painfully across the flat to the opening of the crevice, stood in the shadows.

Over the forest came the long black shape of the Klau raft, the Klau following the chase like a fox-hunter riding to the hounds. The raft came nearer. Barch could see the silhouette of the Klau.

Tick broke out of the forest, ran erratically along the edge of the flat, paused, looked with a passionate eagerness toward the cave. Afraid to come, afraid not to come, thought Barch. Well, give the poor devil a chance. He stepped out. "Hey, Tick." Tick looked up. "Come on."

Tick's face was a mask of indecision. His eyes ran fearfully around the clearing; then overhead came the Klau raft, long and black as a shark. Four Podruods burst out of the forest. Now Tick would have run for the cave but the Podruods cut him off. Barch stood back, silent, his gun ready. The Podruods came at Tick from four directions. Tick stood quiet, and Barch saw his frame grow rigid, his eyes start to pop from their sockets. Look out, Podruods, thought Barch.

Tick ran forward, seemed to run right up the chest of the nearest Podruod. He caught the great red head, set his feet against the chest, performed a peculiar churning motion. The head twisted in three-quarters of a circle; the body fell like a pole. Tick sprang free, raced, dodged, cut in and out. The Podruods lumbered back and forth, finally one caught him by the ankle. Tick fell, doubled up like a squirrel, and with awe Barch saw him catch up the great body, cast it aside as if it were a baseball bat.

Now Tick was caught; Podruods fell on him from all sides; mastiffs tearing at a badger. Tick was down. The Podruods stepped back, their feet swung up, down, with sodden sounds. Barch turned away.

Behind him he felt the pressure of bodies, heard awed murmurings. "Quiet," whispered Barch. "Go up into Big Hole, tell them to be quiet."

The Podruods at last stepped back, looked up at the raft. The Klau stretched lazily, sat up, stared around the flat. His gaze passed over the shadowed crevice; Barch felt the stab of the four-pronged red eyes. The eyes passed on; the bristling black head swung back to inspect the sky.

Black clouds were scudding across Mount Kebali. A few heavy drops of rain spattered on the leaves. The Podruods called up hoarsely, pointing to the clouds. The Klau ignored them. He waved his hand toward the upper valley. The Podruods shuffled sullenly into the forest.

The dead Podruod and the bloody tatter that had been Tick were left on the flat.

Rain started a tentative tattoo on the black fronds — drops big as marbles. The Klau touched a button and a hood snapped over his head. He moved his foot; the raft slid down over the valley.

Barch turned, pushed back into the hall. "That solves the Tick problem."

Chapter XXIII

Komeitk Lelianr sat at the table, studiously intent at the locator — poring over the index, checking into the viewer. Barch stood by the fire, absentmindedly watching the firelight send changing colors across her skin. He tore his glance away. Certainly he wanted to own the creature. Certainly she was a beautiful thing, and she carried his child. But all this was beside the point.

Barch, he said to himself, if there's one thing you've learned beyond anything else, it's that her way of thinking and your way don't mix. Perhaps she, in her turn, had learned that superiority and inferiority were subject to the reference. Perhaps he, by proving the point — at least to his own satisfaction — had divested part of her most urgent attraction.

Still, he thought wistfully, she was an unutterably beautiful thing, and he would have given half his soul to possess her completely. Impossible.

Porridge bounded down the passage into the hall, trotted over to the fire, smelt appreciatively of the pot. Then, with a wary glance at Barch, he went to sit opposite Komeitk Lelianr.

After a moment he spoke to her; she looked up, answered briefly. Porridge darted a glance over his shoulder at Barch, spoke at some length. Barch's curiosity could hold out no longer. He crossed the stone floor, seated himself beside Porridge. "How's the job coming?"

"Very well, very well indeed."

"When do you think you'll be ready?"

Porridge considered. "The deck is finished. Tomorrow we fix on the second barge. Next day we build on a double port. Then you can take the affair into space."

"Is the double port necessary? I'd like to get away from here right away."

"It's indispensable in the event of repair to the drive gear and also when refueling becomes necessary."

"Oh." Barch rubbed his chin. After a moment he said, "Tonight I'll go out after the fuel, and —" he paused, glancing from Komeitk Lelianr back to Porridge. "What's the trouble?"

"Nothing, nothing whatever," said Porridge. He turned ostentatiously away. Komeitk Lelianr returned to the locator.

Barch coldly asked her, "Any luck?"

"No. Nothing definite. I have a tentative idea."

The other Lenape came down from Big Hole, sat in a tight circle at the far bench. Porridge arose and joined them; an immediate clatter of voices arose.

Komeitk Lelianr said hesitantly, "Why are you so anxious to locate the Brain?"

Barch looked her over thoughtfully. "You can't guess?"

"No."

"When I find where it is I'll try to destroy it."

Her eyes jerked up, met his. "Roy — don't you think you should rest tonight?"

"Rest? I've got to get the fuel, *accr*, whatever it's called." He stood up, glanced around the room. Eyes flickered away from his, backs were half-turned. Barch sat down. "What's wrong with everyone?"

Komeitk Lelianr's fingers moved nervously along the locator. "They think — you're tired."

"Tired? Of course I'm tired! Why shouldn't I be tired, and everybody else for that matter? We can rest out in space."

Komeitk Lelianr said in a low voice, "They remember that Clet called you 'Crazy Man'."

Barch sat like an iron statue. "So everybody thinks I'm crazy…I might have known. I saw Porridge giving me a couple wall-eyed looks."

Komeitk Lelianr said in a worried voice, "He can't understand why you want to steal *accr* when there's enough in the cave to last twenty years."

"*Enough to last twenty years!*"

"So he says."

Barch slumped, exhaled a great breath. "Where?"

"In Big Hole. In the crates. Kerbol called it Super."

Barch's face twitched; he could not choose between laughing or yelling. He forced himself to be calm. "I never knew the stuff was *accr*. No one ever told me…Do you think I like ducking around through the fog, getting myself shot up?"

"No," said Komeitk Lelianr hurriedly. "No, no…But why are you so anxious to destroy the Brain?"

Barch, riding a yeasty wave of mingled anger and elation, said, "Think. By now the Brain surely has enough facts to conclude that fugitive slaves are stealing barge-loads of material."

"I suppose so."

"Any day we can expect to be attacked. If I can plant a bomb under the thing, I'll delay this attack a long time."

Komeitk Lelianr frowned. "I don't think you realize the essential nature of Magarak or its organization."

"You've never said a truer word. I feel like a cat in a stamp-mill every time I take out that raft. Look at it this way. Would the Klau be disturbed if I blew up their Brain?"

"I should think so. It would be a most serious matter."

"What's bad for them is good for us. Call it diversionary tactics. That's simple enough. Isn't it?" He took her silence for assent. "Do you think you can find the Brain?"

"I think I've found it."

"Good. And do you still think I'm crazy?"

Her glance went to his left shoulder. "I'm not well-enough acquainted with the norm of your people to judge."

Barch rose to his feet. He said thickly, "About ten more minutes of double-talk, I actually would be crazy."

He went back to the fire. The hell with them all. Explaining motives was useless; his patterns didn't fit their minds. He put his hand to his gun; here was his explanation. He met Komeitk Lelianr's sudden alarmed stare, grimaced. Now she thinks I'm planning to run amok. Very well. No point in explaining anything. Give orders, see that they're obeyed.

He strode across the room to the Lenape. There was a sudden silence; he felt the eyes of the entire tribe on his back.

"Porridge," he said, "you think I'm crazy. That suits me as long as you work; think anything you like. Tomorrow I want you to load Barge No. 3 with all the abiloid we have left, and a couple cases of *accr*. I want you to rig a detonator on the bow, on each forward corner, to go off on contact. I want you to put a cut-out switch in the anti-collision mechanism, so I can disengage it whenever I want. Do you understand?"

Porridge blinked. "Clearly."

"Good." Barch walked across the floor to the entrance, slipped out into the night.

The rain had stopped; the air was strangely calm for the Palkwarkz Ztvo. Barch crossed the clearing, wandered to his raft. For a moment he considered climbing aboard, raising up into the dark sky, riding through the night. But there was no guide-light set out, the locator was in the hall, and once up in the air, he would not be able to find his way back.

He lay on the raft, flat on his back. Never had he known the valley so still. Not a breath of air; not a leaf stirring. He listened. Not a sound. An eery night, fit for strange deeds.

Down the slope near the river came a thud. Barch raised half up on the raft, listened. There was no other sound. He lay back once more... Two more days, then space — wonderful prospect. And then where? Back to Earth? Perhaps he had kept the idea purposely out of his mind. The Earth he would return to would not be the Earth he had left. He might be taken a second time, sent back to Magarak.

Best not think of it. But if the Klau controlled Earth, how would he return? And how tightly, how stringently would they hold it? Could the Earthers resist? And what of the Lekthwans? If Ellen were a typical example, they would be small aid. A cultured people, subtle, artistic, beautiful — but where were they when it came to guts?

Barch chewed his lip. Maybe he was doing the girl an injustice. For instance, he had never heard her complain or whimper. She did her share of the menial jobs. She had the guts, but only in terms of an unyielding stoic characterization. Had they no characterization called *Indomitable Fighter*, or *Unquenchable Resistance*? He'd have to ask Ellen about that.

He considered the future: their child. Who would take charge, who would educate it? He sighed. Ellen, naturally. Would he be allowed paternal privileges, would he ever see this child of his, would Ellen acknowledge him? Barch sighed again. Best not to bring the matter up.

The lights of a barge appeared over Mount Kebali; Barch followed them across the sky, out of sight over Poriflammes Valley. Barch relaxed. Hardly likely that the Klau would come by night. Sometime they must come; why had they delayed so long? The Brain thought sluggishly — or underestimated the urgency of the situation. Barch ruminated, weighing pros and cons.

If the Klau attacked during the next two days, then he would go out to demolish the Brain. If they were able to leave before the Klau acted — so much the better.

Barch swung his feet to the ground, walked out into the open. The strange lull was coming to an end; thunder rattled through the clouds, Barch heard the stealthy patter of rain.

He returned to the cave. As he slid through the crevice he could hear voices raised in heated conversation. He entered the hall. Silence. Faces were pale disks around the room oriented to him like flowers to the sun.

"Go right ahead," said Barch. "Don't mind me."

CHAPTER XXIV

THE KLAU CAME the next day. During the morning Barch mined the bluff, set out his defenses for the flat, but when he looked up and saw the tremendous barge settling easily toward the flat, his heart sank. His preparations suddenly seemed picayune, trivial.

He watched the barge drifting in. It came with ominous ease and certainty, a black monster twice as large as any Barch had seen before. It blotted out half the sky, dropping toward him like a foot coming down on a beetle. Barch jerked back with the impulse to escape.

Spike-haired heads protruded over every rail like an ornamental fringe, and at the stern was a hard-angled shape with the look of lethality.

Barch looked toward the cave; saw a pair of frightened faces peering from the crevice. Flatface came out of the forest, cast a terrified glance over his shoulder, hurried across the flat, humping like a buffalo.

Barch called anxiously, "Hey, Flatface, over here — give me some help." Flatface scuttled only the faster for the cave.

Barch looked after him, seething with fury. Very well, I'll do it myself. He ran through the trees to where four long shapes stood leaning in makeshift troughs — the pipes Pedratz had welded to his order.

The barge was only two hundred feet overhead. Barch jockeyed the trough around, sighted up the pipe into the exposed entrails of the barge. He broke the detonator fuse, jumped back.

There was a dry snap, pop, a rush, a roar. The pipe-rocket split like a starfish; venting blue smoke it whistled erratically up, dodging and twisting. Barch thought, it's a miss, I can't aim these things. But the rocket swerved, caught under the stern, exploded. A hole opened instantly, bodies spattered up, curved out, like drops in a fountain, paused, fell.

The barge sagged down at the stern, spilled its cargo, hung swaying by the bow. Into the flat fell a screaming rain, thrashing, twisting shapes.

Aboard the barge a few still clung to the rails, hanging to each other like a chain of ants. Barch drew his gun, aimed, fired — again, again. The barge was clear of men, except the pilot in the dome, clawing at the controls. But to no avail. Swaying gently the barge sank until the stern touched the ground, and there it stood. Barch shot at the pilot, but the splinter whistled off the dome.

Barch hesitated a moment, then cautiously approached the weapon mounted on the stern. With one eye on the pilot he inspected it, tested the movement. It spun on a swivel. It was a strange pattern, H-shaped with a long central bar, like a naval range-finder. The trigger was in an obvious position. The pilot was climbing out of the dome; no time for niceties of sighting. Barch swung the H around, focussed it as closely as possible, pressed home the trigger. There was a crackling sound; the control dome disappeared. The barge fell flat with a great squash and crush of air.

Barch turned to look at the bodies on the flat. A dozen or so squirmed, one or two crawled moaning along the stone. Barch swung the H, the crackling snapped out; a great oval spot on the flat was gouged out, seared, glossy.

Barch inspected the weapon appreciatively. Somewhere there must be a sighting device — here, a tube, and beside it, a lever.

A thousand feet above floated a raft with a crystal top. Barch peered through the sights. Two rafts. He moved the lever, the two merged. He pressed the trigger. The raft became a few flapping, falling pieces. No more targets. Nothing alive. Barch jumped down to the flat. He looked up to the cave mouth, saw nervous motion inside.

He picked his way among the bodies, slid along the crevice to the hall. The Lenape were huddled into an alcove, like puppies in a basket. "Get busy," snapped Barch. "If you can't fight, you can at least work."

He looked around the hall. Pedratz stood by a wall, his face bland and round as the full moon. "Get your equipment, see if you can cut loose that gun."

The Lenape were trooping up the passage to Big Hole, pressing close together, making nervous motions with their hands. "Porridge," said Barch, "have you fixed up Barge No. 3 as I told you?"

"The work of a moment," said Porridge hastily.

"How much more time before we leave Magarak?"

"Difficult to say. The double port is not yet fabricated; the hull welding will be finished before the day is out."

"Well, hurry up with Barge No. 3. If the Klau start to work on us seriously, we won't last very long. I think I can distract them."

"Dangerous, dangerous."

"Not if you fix everything exactly as I tell you to. Incidentally, you're coming with me. I can't pilot that barge."

Porridge sagged like a loose sack of meal. Without speaking he turned, hurried up the passage.

Barch seated himself at the table across from where Komeitk Lelianr worked at the locator.

"Come to anything definite?"

"Yes, I think so. On the index it's called *Central Organ*."

Barch looked into the viewer, into the jungle of fleshy pastel shapes. The target ring encircled a small green square, surrounded by a blue mass shaped like an ink blot. To one side was a rusty-orange rectangle that seemed to quiver and jump as Barch looked at it; to the other a sprinkle of gray dots. Radiating away from the green square was a series of minute red capillaries, so faint as to be hardly noticeable. "So that's the Brain."

"Nothing else seems likely. I cannot be sure, of course."

"Is it far?"

"It's a third of the way around the planet, in the Central District."

"Central District? More complicated than Quodaras?"

"Quodaras is a newer development, only a few hundred years old."

"Oh. Well, it makes no particular difference."

There was silence for a moment or so. Then, frowning into the viewer, she said, "Roy — do you still think this plan of yours is — feasible?"

Barch made a disgusted sound. "The Klau just lost a barge-load of Podruods. Next time they'll send something heavier. We can't stand up under any serious attack. We've got to get their minds off us long enough to make ourselves scarce. We're walking along a precipice right now. And I've got work to do. I've got to see that there's enough raw material aboard for the sustenators. I've got to get Barge No. 3 loaded with abiloid — and a couple crates of *accr*."

The day passed for Barch like the day before his execution, each second, each minute stretched far out, the hours paradoxically compressed.

The work moved with exasperating slowness; Barch ducked back and forth into Big Hole, standing fretfully over the Lenape, convinced of their inefficiency but unable to comment because he did not understand what they were doing. He barked at the women who were carrying domestic utensils into the barge, raged at Flatface and the labor crew for spending their time gaping at the field of Podruod corpses instead of carrying aboard the logs of green timber they had cut.

Pedratz successfully cut loose the heavy weapon on the stern of the war-barge. Barch carried it slung under the raft to a niche just inside the cave mouth; from here he could command almost the whole of the valley. Suppose the Klau came while he was off on his final mission? He called to Chevrr, the dour Splang. "Come over here a minute."

Chevrr approached suspiciously. Barch explained the working of the gun to him, made Chevrr focus on several objects near and far to his satisfaction.

"Now you stay up here. You're the guard. If you see the Klau coming, don't shoot, call for me. If I'm not here, use your own discretion."

Chevrr made a sound of acquiescence. Barch strode through the hall, climbed the passage into Big Hole.

Porridge was standing beside Barge No. 3, looking up at the dome lackadaisically. "Porridge!" barked Barch. The Lenape turned his head; the round opal eyes met Barch's hot hazel eyes without expression. "When are you going to have that barge ready?"

"It's all ready now."

"Oh," said Barch. "The explosive aboard?"

"Everything."

"Two cases of *accr*?"

"Correct. The rest is loaded aboard the space-hull."

"Good. Now you're sure you've done what I wanted?"

"There is a detonator fixed at each corner of the bow, connected to the cargo."

"Good. I'll get the men to open out the cave, then we'll be off."

Porridge made a vague whining sound. "I do not care to go. The journey is unnecessary."

Barch's face muscles twitched. He controlled his temper. "Show me how to operate the barge."

Porridge jumped with great eagerness aboard. "It is very simple. Here is the speed. To go anywhere on the planet, set the target on the locator, throw this switch. This ball controls the barge when the locator-guide is not in operation." He spoke on, touching knobs and bars and finger-guides. Barch asked questions, sat in the seat, made sure he understood.

He climbed back down to the ground. "I'll go get the men to take down the wall; you bring the barge out through the hole."

Barch stood in the flat watching the rocks fall away from the opening. A black aperture appeared. Chevrr yelled down, a hoarse cry, "The Klau!"

The men at the mouth to Big Hole froze; Barch looked up. Slipping down over Mount Kebali came a great black ship.

Hysterical wailing broke out everywhere around the cave — loud sobs of mortal unabashed fear. "Shut up!" yelled Barch. "Get inside the cave!"

Barch took Chevrr's place at the gun, crouching behind the edge of the rock.

The ship cruised easily down the valley, past the flat, then rose over the narrow mouth, circled, came slowly back. The aperture into Big Hole was in shadow, facing away from the valley; it would hardly attract attention.

The ship once more passed before the flat. A great crackling filled the air; the flat jarred, shimmered. The crackling ceased. The wrecked barge, the Podruod corpses were gone. Barch's diaphragm convulsed.

The crackling sounded again. The forest below the flat collapsed. Once more. The rock by Barch's face quivered. Behind, in the cave, the wailing recommenced. Barch growled over his shoulder, "Stop that racket!" He turned back. So far no harm done; they were shooting at random. Only a lucky shot could hurt them. He hoped the Klau commander would come to the same conclusion.

The ship passed almost overhead; Barch followed it in the gunsights. Perhaps the hull was proof to this relatively feeble piece; he held his fire.

The Klau commander acted as Barch had hoped. The ship circled down the valley once again, paused over the commanding bluff, settled slowly.

In high excitement Barch ran into the cave. "Porridge! Where's Porridge?"

Komeitk Lelianr, sitting at the table, pointed to an alcove. Barch ran over to find the Lenape wound together in a tight sweating ball. "Porridge, get out of there!" He reached in with his good hand, tore the cluster of bodies apart. Porridge's red blinking face appeared. "Come out of there. Hurry!"

Porridge struggled clear.

"Get to that remote-control box. When I give you the word — let go the No. 1. Understand?"

Porridge shuffled to the box on the back table, Barch returned to the crevice.

The ship alighted softly on the bluff; instantly a ramp fell down, a corps of Podruods sprang out. Barch ducked back into the cave. "Now!"

Violet light flashed through the crevice; an instant later the face of the cliff rang as if with the impact of shrapnel.

Barch cautiously peered out across the valley. The bluff was gouged and splintered; in the valley below were the broken pieces of the warship.

Barch pushed back into the cave. "Porridge, where are you?" He ran across the room, caught the chunky shoulders. "Back to work. We count our time in minutes now." He swung around. "Ellen!"

"Yes?"

"I'm going now."

"Roy —"

"Don't argue with me. If I don't go, we have three or four hours of life ahead of us. They'll take us seriously now, they'll do the job right — unless I get in the first lick."

"But, Roy, the ship must be almost ready…"

"Keep Porridge busy until I get back. It's the only way to give us a few hours grace."

"And if you don't come back?"

"I'll come back. But if I don't —" he paused "— good-by."

"Good-by."

Barch hesitated an instant; suddenly there were a thousand things to tell her. She turned away quickly.

Barch ran up the passage into Big Hole. "Porridge, climb into that barge, back it out, push open a hole."

Porridge wordlessly climbed into the dome. The stern of the barge brushed the wall; it fell open. The barge slid out into the air.

Barch stood a moment looking at the sky. Twilight was falling through the valley. Overhead the sky was mottled, like watered gray silk. The trees stood quiet and still; there was no sound. Barch's voice sounded loud. "Sure you won't come with me, Porridge?"

Porridge shuffled his feet. "I am needed to work."

"Very well. Work hard."

"We will be done soon."

Barch jumped into the little raft, slid it up to the cat-walk behind the control dome. He looked into the hold, saw a satisfactory bulk of boxes. "Enough to do a little damage, eh, Porridge?" he called down jocularly.

Porridge threw up his hands, walked away.

Barch looked around the flat, looked up to the sky. In the cave mouth he saw a slim slight figure. Ellen? He waved. The shape vanished within.

Barch entered the control dome, seated himself in the unfamiliar seat. Gingerly he put into practice Porridge's instructions. The barge rose vertically up. Barch twisted the locator index, looking into the viewer. There — a green square on an irregular blue shape. But before he snapped the switch he manipulated the controls to get the feel of the barge. Up, down, sideways, ahead, turn. Nothing too difficult. Barch snapped the switch on the automatic pilot, pushed home the speed button, sat back.

Chapter XXV

THE BARGE SLIPPED like a shadow over Mount Kebali. Ahead was Quodaras District, a horizon-to-horizon blur of light. Below the stone quarry showed a lonesome cluster of lights; how long ago it seemed that he and Kerbol had slid down to waylay Tick. Tick was dead, Kerbol was dead: fruitless, unsatisfactory, curtailed lives.

The stone quarry vanished astern like a pearl in the fog. Below Barch saw the glimmer of the Tchul Sea, the reflection from the far band of lights glistening on the surface.

The barge suddenly slipped sideways, steadied; Barch realized that now he moved in a traffic stream. Other barges floated past, alongside, over. Incurious faces showed dimly: faces with dead souls.

The barge flew over the glaring lights, the fiery pots, the churning arms, the incalculable shapes of Magarak.

Suddenly it occurred to him, how would he find his way home? There was no locator on the raft. He must remember to unclip it, take it with him.

On the locator he gauged the progress of his voyage. Not yet halfway to Central Organ. Below, the buildings, the shapes, the moving arms, the fantastic fires, took on proportions more enormous than he had yet seen. The air reeked with acrid odors; the clatter and jangle of the processes reached up to astonish him. How could men survive such a nightmare?

And yet men did survive. Men had survived ice-ages, pestilences, wars, and they survived Magarak. Human will to live approached the infinite. And Barch thought, put the Zulu buck — (odd, he had not thought of the Zulu for a long time) — put the Zulu buck at a modern city intersection, and the Zulu might also wonder at man's resistance to self-created hell. Barch wondered idly, suppose you brought the Zulu to Magarak, what then? His imagination rejected the idea.

He sank back into the seat, feeling strangely at peace. The chips were down; the hay was in the barn. His problems were behind him now; no more straining or worry. He either succeeded in his mission, returned to the cave, and left Magarak behind — or he died.

For a few minutes he lay drowsily back in the seat, then bestirred himself, checked distances in the locator. Two-thirds of the distance. He looked behind. Lights, swinging black shapes blurred in the distance. The same to all sides, all around the horizon. Without the locator he would be lost. He made an urgent mental note: remember the locator.

Minutes passed; Barch began to grow tense. Easy, he told himself. Either you do or you don't.

At the extreme edge of the locator the green square became visible. Barch looked ahead. There — that tall blocky tower, that irregular bluish shape.

Barch snapped off the locator, pulled the speed-control out to slow, dropped to a lower level. The tower soared above him, and Barch saw that it indeed glowed faintly green.

He started a circle, carefully threading the vertical avenues and lanes. Barges cut across his course; he caught the flash of startled faces. Easy, Barch, watch what you are doing. You don't want to meet any traffic cops now.

At the foot of the tower, he saw a wide opening — a ground-level landing deck.

He lowered the barge. A raft with a crystal dome drew alongside; Barch could see the pilot peering curiously in his direction. Barch paid no heed. The raft drifted reluctantly away.

A vast sound like a siren rattled the air. Alarm? Danger signal? Barch raised in his seat, looked in all directions. Nothing untoward seemed under way.

The ground was close; the opening, lit by greenish-yellow light, was on his level. He flicked off the anti-collision circuit; started the barge toward the opening. Slowly, give him time to get clear. He watched a moment. Dead center. Good.

He opened the door, clambered back to his raft, climbed aboard. He stopped; my God, the locator. He ran back. The hole was very close. With his one hand he fumbled with the clips. One came loose, then the other. He caught it under his arm, sprinted back. The hole almost engulfed him. Aboard the raft, cast loose, away…

The air bit into his face; he hunched down, urging the raft ahead. Faster, faster. Better lie flat. He fell forward on his face.

Light splattered the sky, painted the overcast dazzling violet-white. Ah, thought Barch, the explosion. Success. He clung to the raft. Faster, faster.

There came a great wind, lifting the raft like a chip on the surf, flung it high and miles ahead. Barch glimpsed the great tower toppling, falling, smashing. There came a second explosion. Barch saw a blue blast, a tremendous fan-shaped flare, reaching instantaneously up, breaking through the overcast. Where the tower stood was a seething puddle of lava. The massive structures beside were mangled, torn awry, and as the great blue blast quietly died, the buildings glowed red and slumped.

The second air-wave caught Barch now, a milder, sharper impact, one which he heard as sound. Looking behind once more he wondered how many people had died, how many Klau, how many slaves. The Klau — Barch shrugged. The slaves — death was small loss to the slaves.

The raft was riding on an even keel, under control. Barch looked into the locator — peered in astonishment. The viewer showed blackness, nothing. Barch shook it, pounded it to no avail.

In sudden thought he looked behind. Did the Central Organ control the locator? In disgust and panic he tossed the mechanism behind him. He looked ahead. How had he come? Was this the right direction? All directions looked alike. There was no moon, no stars.

He looked over the side, searching for some half-noticed landmark. The buildings bulged up, the myriad lights and vast motions were the same.

He looked behind. The tower was gone. But — there was something subtly different about the approach. Barch got the raft around, circled to the left, looking toward the former tower. Building planes shifted, flares and fires took on different patterns. Now, this looked right. It was a gamble — but the whole exploit had been a gamble. So far he had won.

Barch turned the raft away from the tower, set out at full speed.

Now the minutes dragged where before they had sped. Surely he had not been so long over these monstrous shapes, with the bristling trusses like moth antenna. He kept on. The buildings seemed to diminish. But by now he should be nearing Tchul Sea. There was no Tchul Sea in sight. He had gone wrong. Now — turn to the right or turn to the left? No. Straight ahead, another ten minutes. With anxiety gnawing at him, one minute was like ten minutes. In every direction sprawled the man-hating bulk of Magarak.

He had come wrong. And yet — a few more miles. And what was that vague blankness ahead? *Thalasse, thalasse!* had shouted Xenophon's myriad. The sea! muttered Barch. Good old Tchul Sea!

The mud flats gleaming with murky phosphorescence like dead fish passed below; ahead was the mass of the Palamkum. It was almost like home, thought Barch. Now rest. His fingers relaxed. If they spent five years in space, he'd sleep the first year. Rest, sleep. No more driving, no more plotting and planning.

Below passed the lonely lights of the stone quarry; there was the ridge of Mount Kebali. He slid down the long slant into Palkwarkz Ztvo, noticing that there was grayness in the sky. Had the night passed so soon?

There was the blasted bluff, there the seared flat, there the black opening into Big Hole.

Barch landed the raft, jumped to the ground, ran up the hill toward the cave mouth. He whistled in case anyone should be on guard, but there was no challenge.

He reached the crevice, stopped short. He frowned. Where was the thin trickle of firelight that always glowed from the gap? Had they let the fire die? Had they extinguished the lamps?

He stepped into the hall. The hearth glowed with dull coals. "Hey," Barch cried out. "Is everybody dead?"

No response, no whisper, no murmur, no slightest stir of sound. Barch ran up the passage into Big Hole. Gray light poured in through the opening. The double-barge was gone. Big Hole was empty.

Barch walked slowly to the opening. Wide. He looked up into the sky. The overcast came racing fast across Mount Kebali.

He returned to the hall, sat on the bench, held his hand to his head. The coals glowed, winked, and one by one died out. Barch sat in the cool silence.

Gray light seeped in through the crevice. Barch rose, went slowly outside. He banged the stump of his left arm on the stone and felt no pain. "Well," said Barch aloud, "so much for that."

CHAPTER XXVI

BARCH STOOD in the cave opening. Light rain fell slanting down the wind, so cold as to be near-sleet; perhaps the Magarak winter was beginning. Purple-gray overcast, heavy and twisted as brains, scraped the black ridges. The notch at the mouth of the valley was blurred; the black fronds of the forest shook and rattled.

He returned inside the cave, threw wood on the coals, watched the smoulder start up into little flames, grow to a blaze.

He turned away, and without reason climbed the passage into Big Hole. Watery gray light entered through the gap, twenty feet high, fifty feet wide; he could not possibly fill it in alone. He shrugged, turned away, looked around the cavern.

He was still lord of vast properties — the cargo of sustenators, less the three for the ship and two in the hall. There were crates of welding tape, the igniter, the cutting tools, spools of cable, a respectable pile of decking. The explosives were used up, all the *accr* had gone with the double-barge. Oddments, scrap, broken crates littered the uneven half of the floor. Nothing of value or immediate usefulness.

Barch started back down to the hall, then stopped. Something had to be done about the hole. With only one hand, piling up a wall of rocks was out of the question. But he could rig a makeshift screen, lashing up the deck-sheets with cable and maybe throwing a few branches against the outside for camouflage.

He returned to the hall, fed himself from the sustenator. The fire was warm, the rain hissed outside. He felt drowsy, torpid. He dozed for a few moments, then awoke with a start. Voices? Sweet woman-voices? Heart thumping like a hammer, he jumped up, peered around the hall.

Nothing. He looked down the back passage, listened. Silence. He went out to the crevice, scanned the sky. The rain had become a heavy lashing torrent; the black fronds bowed, shivered; the forest sighed, wind moaned down the valley.

Barch went up to Big Hole, worked furiously, half in the rain, half out. When he had finished, a double row of panels hung across the hole, flapping and bumping. Not good, but better than nothing.

He went back to the hall, sat staring into the fire, and so the day passed.

On the fourth morning, overcome by restlessness, he took up the raft. He landed precariously on the summit of Mount Kebali, stood looking out across Quodaras District. A smell of smoke hung in the air. Along the horizon Barch saw no less than twenty plumes of leaden vapor sweeping down the dank wind. As he watched a star-shaped flash of red fire burst up in the middle distance. Half a minute later, he felt a dull shock on his face, heard a rumble like thunder. Resisting the temptation to fly out over the city, Barch returned to the cave.

He spent half a day piling fronds of vegetation against the Big Hole panels. Backing off to inspect his work, he saw a barge sliding down into the valley.

Barch ran to the cave mouth, ducked behind his gun. He sighted through the finder; his hand went to the trigger…He frowned, squinted. These were no Podruods; in fact, there were women standing at the rail as well as men. Fifty or sixty of them, a bedraggled lot, apparently all of the same race, with skin and features not unlike his own.

The barge settled to the flat. The stairs snapped out, a thin bald man with a shrewd round face jumped to the ground, followed by a tall youth with short dark hair. Barch could hear the voices, but not the words.

After a moment the rest of the passengers climbed down the ladder, stood looking uncertainly around the flat. The thin bald man spied Barch and the gun. He crouched. The others, following his gaze, froze in consternation, their voices dwindled.

Barch called out in the Magarak pidgin-tongue, "Come up here where I can talk to you." The thin bald man and the dark-haired youth approached warily. "What brings you here?" Barch asked gruffly.

The thin man looked carefully behind Barch into the crevice. "You might call us fugitives. What about you?"

"The same."

The dark-haired youth said quietly aside, "If wild men come any wilder, let's go back to Podinsiras where it's safe."

"Might be he's a little off his rocker."

Barch smiled bitterly. "I speak English myself."

The newcomers stared at him.

"Forget it," said Barch wearily. "So I am a wild man; so I am off my rocker." He nodded toward the barge. "All of you from Earth?"

"We're what's left of Oakville, Iowa."

"Never heard of it."

"The Klau dropped an army around town, herded us into their ship. This was two, three months ago. What's been going on since, we don't know; the slave revolt gave us a chance to bust loose."

"Slave revolt?"

"Yep, started about four days ago. Somebody blew up the main headquarters with most of the Klau big shots. Ever since Magarak's been a madhouse."

"Well, well," said Barch. "And now what do you intend to do?"

"Well," said the thin man, "we figured we'd try to get back to Earth by hook or by crook. My name's Smith, by the way; this is my son Tim."

"I'm Roy Barch."

Smith gestured to the barge. "I understand these things run on the same principle as the space-ships — grab at space and pull themselves along. Now if maybe we could make one of these air-tight —"

Barch sat down on a rock, ran his hand through his hair.

"What's the matter?" asked the thin man. "Did I say something wrong?"

"No," said Barch. "It's just that you've come to the right place. I organize these parties. I'm a specialist on them." He heaved a deep sigh. "You really want to leave Magarak?"

"Naturally."

"You're willing to work, take a few risks, maybe —" Barch held up the stump of his left arm.

"Yes!"

"All right, you've got a partner. Let's get busy. Take your barge around the corner. I'll let down the sheets, we'll slide it into the Big Hole."

Barch jumped to his feet. Smith and his son Tim backed away a little.

"I'm harmless," said Barch. "Just anxious. This time I'll do it right."

"Sure, sure," said Smith soothingly.

"Tonight we go out stealing. I know the routine cold. First we get the *accr* at the quarry. Next we go after Lenape and the sustenators… But we've already got plenty sustenators and we can do without the Lenape…On second thought we need a few Lenape. Something might go wrong with the inner workings en route and none of us could fix it."

Smith asked anxiously, "You feeling all right, son?"

"I feel fine," said Barch. "Let's get busy."

Double-Ark II rose into the twilight. Barch looked down into Palkwarkz Ztvo, hating the black forest, the black mountains, the interminable drizzle. And yet — he looked along the length of the valley — he had experienced a great deal here; he had accomplished much. "Wish I had a photograph of the place," he said over his shoulder to Tim.

Tim clutched his arm. "Look."

Barch twisted sharply. Through the clouds flickered a dozen long dark shapes. The overcast swirled aside for an instant; the shapes showed as long torpedoes. The overcast closed; the shapes were gone.

"Those weren't Klau ships," said Barch thoughtfully.

"No, I guess not."

"I thought I saw some kind of emblem on the first one."

Tim hesitated. "I did too. But I think I was wrong. It couldn't be what I thought it was."

"United Nations emblem?"

"But it couldn't be."

"No. It couldn't be…Of course we were building space-ships, but — it's impossible."

CHAPTER XXVII

THERE WAS A KNOCK on the door of Barch's room in the St. Francis Hotel. Barch looked up from the newspaper. "Who is it?"

"Tim Smith."

Barch rose to his feet. "If it's a reporter, I'll break your neck."

He swung open the door. Tim Smith came in. "Just me."

Barch looked up and down the corridor, shut and locked the door. "I've been besieged the last couple days." He rapped the newspaper with the back of his hand. "I'd like to know how this stuff got out."

Tim Smith picked it up.

RAZING OF ENEMY WAR INDUSTRIES
REACHES HALFWAY MARK

"Is that what you're talking about?"

"No," said Barch. "This feature article, by-lined Cyril Heats." He took the newspaper. "Listen."

> The break-up of the Klau Empire under the pounding of the Great Lenau-Lekthwan-Earth-Bakaima Coalition is now history, and Earthmen will always glory in the fact that their fledgling Space-Navy dealt the first effective blow against the Klau slave-worlds.
>
> As a significant sidelight to this tremendous epoch in our history comes the news that one Roy Barch of San Francisco, captured by the Klau five years ago, can claim the honor of being the first Earthman to strike back at the Klau.

A few days ago the epic four-year voyage of the Double-Ark II was chronicled on these pages. Readers will remember that a heroic group of Earthmen, enslaved during the original Klau raids, won back to Earth in a makeshift space-ship. It has now been revealed that the great Magarak slave revolt, which contributed so strikingly to the success of the original Punitive Expedition, was the result of Barch's one-man assault against the Klau...

Barch threw down the paper. "It goes on from there. Barch this, Barch that!" He ran his hand through his hair. "What beats me is, how did it get out?"

"Somebody must have spilled the beans," said Tim blandly.

Barch darted him a keen look. "I've already got an idea of who I can thank."

"I wanted to make sure you got what was coming to you," said Tim. "Keys to the city, gold-plated hook for your trick arm, a Roy Barch Memorial..."

Barch glared.

"Take it easy," said Tim. "You know you love it."

Barch laughed. "It might get me a job. I borrowed five hundred bucks from my uncle. He said it was all my own fault, that I never should have fooled around the Lekthwans to begin with."

"Speaking of Lekthwans," said Smith, "look at this." He pointed to an article low on the page.

"I saw it," said Barch.

The helicopter landed on the terrace of dark blue glass. Barch jumped out. "I won't be too long," he told the pilot.

The pilot lit a cigarette. "Take your time; you're paying for it."

Barch walked slowly around the terrace. To his right was the rococo balustrade of blue and white striped glass; to the left rose the crystal walls apparently so transparent, so confusing to the eye. It was very familiar; but it looked small, like a scene remembered from childhood, and a little dreary.

He passed by the alcove which had housed Markel's air-boat. There was the boat, shining and glistening as if Barch and Claude Darran had only just finished polishing it.

He went on. There — on that very spot Claude Darran's body had lain. And there — he looked up. Approaching was a young Lekthwan, gold skin splendid in the sunlight. He wore black trousers, a soft black cloak and cap. Many times Barch had seen Markel in the same garb; it gave him a curious pang of timelessness.

The Lekthwan halted in front of Barch. "Why are you here?" he asked courteously.

Barch said, "I might ask the same of you." Same insufferable Lekthwan superiority, he thought. Somehow it had lost the power to do more than irk him.

The Lekthwan bowed slightly. "I am Acting Commissioner for Sector Commerce."

"Who is Commissioner?"

"There has been no full Commissioner since Tkz Maerkl-Elaksd."

Barch said slowly, "I came up for two reasons. I left some belongings here five years ago."

The Lekthwan frowned. "Incomprehensible…Five years ago Tkz Maerkl-Elaksd was in residence."

"That's correct, but it doesn't matter. The second reason is coming up now."

The Lekthwan turned. "The ship from home," he murmured. "Please excuse me; can you come some other day?"

"No," said Barch. He went to lean on the balustrade…Five years ago he had stood here watching a great vivid ball come rushing up to the terrace. And just so had the ball locked to the landing stage, just so had a child run forth, just so had Komeitk Lelianr stepped out on the dark blue glass.

There were changes. The child was a boy, and his skin was a pale clear gold. Komeitk Lelianr was quieter, thoughtful, though she looked a little older. And Barch's heart had not been pounding then as it was now.

She saw Barch immediately; indeed her eyes swept the terrace as if she were seeking him. She stopped in midstride. Her mouth tightened; Barch saw her eyebrows and eyelashes move in a quick series of characterizations.

She hesitated only an instant, then walked over to the balustrade. "I had not expected to see you here, Roy."

"I suppose not."

"You look very well... How long have you been home?"

"About two weeks. How about you?"

She spoke in a careful voice. "We made a fast voyage; eight months. The Lenape were able to work out a space-drive."

"We had no Lenape. We were all Earthmen."

"Oh? Then how did you find your way home?"

"By a very simple means. Perhaps it may strike you as primitive. After we left Magarak we searched the sky. In one direction, in only one direction could we expect to find familiar constellations: in the direction diametrically across the Sun from Magarak. We found Orion, very small, very faint. We started in that direction, and kept on going."

"That's very ingenious... I was sure you would get home."

Barch smiled grimly. "I was never quite so sure."

She looked out into the warm air, hazy with afternoon vapor. "I feel I must explain to you —"

"Forget it," said Barch. "I know all about it. It wasn't your idea. The Lenape said, 'The crazy man is gone; now is a good time, we'll escape him and his mad ideas as well as the Klau,' and everybody thought it was a good idea."

"No," she said. "Not I."

"No. You kept your mouth shut. It was none of your concern, you told yourself. But you did have qualms. You hesitated. And they said, 'Hurry, are you coming or not?' And you went."

Her eyes were still searching the hazy distances. The little boy came up to her; absently she stroked his hair. "That's very close... I realized that I owed you my life, but on Magarak my life was worth nothing to me; and I owed you nothing. I realize now that I owe you my freedom, and now my life and freedom are very precious." She turned, met his eyes. Barch fascinatedly watched the shift of her eyebrows. "And I will pay, in whatever way I can."

Barch smiled. "What's the name of this characterization?"

Her mouth set angrily. "I mean it."

Barch shook his head. "You owe me nothing. My motives in protecting you, in trying to leave Magarak were completely selfish."

"Nevertheless — I profited, and you lost. I must make adjustment."

"Adjustment?" He eyed her speculatively. "Exactly how do you mean, adjustment?"

"I can give you money."

Barch nodded. "I suppose you could."

She looked to where the young Acting Commissioner conferred with a tall majestic Lekthwan in a claret-red cloak. "If you cared to come to Lekthwa — to study, or for curiosity — you would be the guest of myself and of my people for as long as you liked."

"No, thanks. I've had enough space-travel. I'm glad to be home."

Her skin coppered with blood. "This obligation weighs me down; I must rid myself of it!"

"Well, what's next on the list?"

She looked up full into his eyes. "If you want me, I will be your mate, your wife." The words seemed to push themselves through her lips.

Barch grunted. "No thanks. Five years ago I learned the hard way. I sure did."

"That was Magarak, when I had no choice."

"What's the difference? If I wanted to marry, I'd want a wife, not a white elephant. We'd never be happy together. We don't think alike. You're contemptuous of my race. Here on Earth, we're learning to beat prejudice; you've got that still ahead of you. How would I feel married to a woman who's ashamed to introduce me to my own son?"

Komeitk Lelianr very deliberately turned to the little boy, spoke in Lekthwan. He turned, looked at Barch with a new look of wonder and awe. Barch patted his head. "Poor kid, there's no point dragging him into this mess…There's no mess anyway. Even on the improbable assumption that I loved and respected you, we have nothing in common. Our people have nothing in common. You've gained your plateau, you live beautiful lives. We're still working. I hope we never hit this plateau; I hope there's always enough tribulation and grief and confusion to keep us sweating and cursing each other." He looked down at the little boy. "What's your name, young fellow?"

Komeitk Lelianr said hurriedly, "He doesn't understand English."

"I suppose you're fitting him out with a hundred different personalities."

Komeitk Lelianr's jaw set. "I am teaching him to be a Lekthwan."

Barch grinned. "Don't worry. You've suffered for him, he's yours… Well, enough of this. I'll pack up my gear and move on."

She looked up at him intently. "You've changed a great deal, Roy."

"I suppose I have."

"But in some ways you remain the same."

"How so?"

"When we first met, you didn't like the Lekthwans."

"No." Barch looked back along the avenues of the past. "I had a sneaking hunch that they might be right when they claimed to be superior, and it hurt my vanity. Now I know better. I don't have any personal feeling either for or against Lekthwans. We're all humans…Oh, I've changed all right."

"Perhaps I've changed too."

"But you're still a Lekthwan and I'm an Earther."

"You seem a great deal more conscious of the fact than I."

Barch started to protest, then caught himself up short. Perhaps he had not changed so much in five years as he had thought. "Human minds are just too damn complex," he said inconsequentially.

Komeitk Lelianr shrugged; she seemed to have lost interest in the conversation.

Barch asked stiffly, "How long do you stay on Earth?"

"Only a day or so. I came for my father's belongings."

"And then?"

"And then — I will go back to Lekthwa." She spoke listlessly. "It is not the home I remembered…Somewhere I have caught a strange uneasiness. I have been excited talking to you." She looked thoughtfully up into his face.

He turned away. "I'll pick up my gear and be off."

She said nothing. He took a step away. "Good-by."

"Good-by, Roy."

He walked swiftly to the little room he had shared with Claude Darran. It was quite empty. Nothing I wanted anyway, thought Barch.

He returned to the terrace. Komeitk Lelianr still stood leaning back with her elbows on the balustrade. She was looking at him; she radiated an attraction, a new-physical force that impelled him toward her. He took a short step forward, halted. She looked at him with a curious expression neither inviting nor forbidding. Barch took a deep breath.

"Good-by, Ellen."

"Good-by, Roy."

He ran to the helicopter, jumped in. The pilot was reading a magazine.

"Let's go," said Barch.

The pilot stretched languidly. "Finish so soon?"

"Finish?" muttered Barch. "What do you mean 'finish'? There's nothing in life that has a finish."

"You're beyond me there, mister."

"Let's go," said Barch shortly.

The pilot looked down the terrace. "That young lady is coming down this way."

Barch slowly stepped out of the cab. He saw that she was breathing very hard. Her mouth was firm, pale, tight.

"Well?"

"I don't want you to leave."

"But—"

"Roy—it's taking a chance. I'm willing if you are."

He made no pretense of misunderstanding. "A big chance. You'll be cut off from your people."

"Perhaps, perhaps not...Are you afraid?"

Barch looked at her long seconds. Something warm broke inside him. "No. I'm not afraid."

Jack Vance was born in 1916 to a well-off California family that, as his childhood ended, fell upon hard times. As a young man he worked at a series of unsatisfying jobs before studying mining engineering, physics, journalism and English at the University of California Berkeley. Leaving school as America was going to war, he found a place as an ordinary seaman in the merchant marine. Later he worked as a rigger, surveyor, ceramicist, and carpenter before his steady production of sf, mystery novels, and short stories established him as a full-time writer.

His output over more than sixty years was prodigious and won him three Hugo Awards, a Nebula Award, a World Fantasy Award for lifetime achievement, as well as an Edgar from the Mystery Writers of America. The Science Fiction and Fantasy Writers of America named him a grandmaster and he was inducted into the Science Fiction Hall of Fame.

His works crossed genre boundaries, from dark fantasies (including the highly influential *Dying Earth* cycle of novels) to interstellar space operas, from heroic fantasy (the *Lyonesse* trilogy) to murder mysteries featuring a sheriff (the Joe Bain novels) in a rural California county. A Vance story often centered on a competent male protagonist thrust into a dangerous, evolving situation on a planet where adventure was his daily fare, or featured a young person setting out on a perilous odyssey over difficult terrain populated by entrenched, scheming enemies.

Late in his life, a world-spanning assemblage of Vance aficionados came together to return his works to their original form, restoring material cut by editors whose chief preoccupation was the page count of a pulp magazine. The result was the complete and authoritative *Vance Integral Edition* in 44 hardcover volumes. Spatterlight Press is now publishing the VIE texts as ebooks, and as print-on-demand paperbacks.

Colophon

This book was printed using Adobe Arno Pro as the primary text font, with NeutraFace used on the cover.

This title was created from the digital archive of the Vance Integral Edition, a series of 44 books produced under the aegis of the author by a worldwide group of his readers. The VIE project gratefully acknowledges the editorial guidance of Norma Vance, as well as the cooperation of the Department of Special Collections at Boston University, whose John Holbrook Vance collection has been an important source of textual evidence.

Special thanks to R.C. Lacovara, Patrick Dusoulier, Koen Vyverman, Paul Rhoads, Chuck King, Gregory Hansen, Suan Yong, and Josh Geller for their invaluable assistance preparing final versions of the source files.

Digitize: Richard Chandler, John A. Schwab; Format: R.C. Lacovara; Diff: Richard Chandler, David A. Kennedy; Tech Proof: Lawrence Schick; Text Integrity: David A. Kennedy, Steve Sherman, Tim Stretton; Implement: John McDonough, Hans van der Veeke; Security: Paul Rhoads; Compose: John A. Schwab; Comp Review: Andreas Björklind, Marcel van Genderen, Charles King, Robin L. Rouch; Update Verify: Top Changwatchai, John A. D. Foley, Rob Friefeld, David A. Kennedy, Charles King, Paul Rhoads, Robin L. Rouch; RTF-Diff: Charles King, Robin L. Rouch; Textport: Patrick Dusoulier, Suan Hsi Yong; Proofread: Brian Bieniowski, Karl Kellar, Ken Kellett, R.C. Lacovara, Bob Luckin, Jim Pattison, Joel Riedesel, Robin L. Rouch, Jeffrey Ruszczyk, Steve Sherman, Gan Uesli Starling

Artwork (maps based on original drawings by Jack and Norma Vance):

Paul Rhoads, Christopher Wood

Book Composition and Typesetting: Joel Anderson

Art Direction and Cover Design: Howard Kistler

Proofing: Christian J. Corley, Steve Sherman

Jacket Blurb: Steve Sherman, John Vance

Management: John Vance, Koen Vyverman